DARK WHISPERS

A DR HARRISON LANE MYSTERY
BOOK 8

GWYN BENNETT

Storm
PUBLISHING

Ebook ISBN: 978-1-80508-028-2
Paperback ISBN: 978-1-80508-029-9

Cover design: Tash Webber
Cover images: Alamy, Shutterstock

Published by Storm Publishing.
For further information, visit:
www.stormpublishing.co

ALSO BY GWYN BENNETT

The Dr Harrison Lane Mysteries

1. *Broken Angels*

2. *Beautiful Remains*

3. *Deadly Secrets*

4. *Innocent Dead*

5. *Perfect Beauties*

6. *Captive Heart*

7. *Winter Graves*

8. *Dark Whispers*

9. *Burning Lies*

The DI Clare Falle Series

1. *Lonely Hearts*

2. *Home Help*

3. *Death Bond*

The Villagers

1

The forest reminded Justin Protheroe of the sea from his childhood home in Scotland. There were days when it was calm, beautiful, and serene, a welcoming natural environment that relaxed and soothed him. Then, there were the days when it seemed to take on its own peculiar personality; one that was angry and hostile, putting him on edge. Today was one of those days.

He'd brought Barney, their black Labrador, for a good run after two days of rain had kept their walks short. Justin usually loved the forest, but today the trees seemed to have an agenda all their own. Whispering and moaning to each other, their branches bent and shivered conspiratorially. Bark rubbed and creaked high above his head, sharing their secrets amongst themselves. Even the birds seemed to have sensed an unwelcoming presence and disappeared off to a more hospitable place. Justin was a sensible man, not usually prone to imaginative thoughts, but some kind of sixth sense had set off his fight or flight response and it was making him feel uneasy.

It had started with the figure he thought he saw, running between the trees a few hundred yards away. It had been fleeting and almost ghostlike. A black shadow of a person who melted into the dark heart of the woodland, swallowed into its belly like it belonged. It wasn't as if they never saw anybody else on these walks. The forest was big, but he'd often bumped into other walkers or horse riders following the wide paths. Yet this figure had been different.

Barney showed no hint of having picked up on what his master had seen. Didn't they say dogs and animals were good at sensing danger? Or had an over-indulged pet Labrador lost his natural instincts for anything other than rooting out sausages and the warm spot on the sofa?

Justin was aware of the revival of a local folk story which told of a wolfman creature in the forest. Half man, half canine. Perhaps that had somehow infected his subconscious. There had even been eyewitness drawings of this so-called wolfman, which ran silently through the trees, upright and with a body and head like a human, but covered in black hair. Recently a sheep had been found dismembered, the carcass stripped of the most edible meat. Human footprints had been discovered in the area and people swore to having caught glimpses of the frightening wolf-like man in the trees. The local paper had run a whole feature on the stories, and it had provided content for the letters page and website comments for weeks after. Justin hadn't believed a word of it. It might sell papers but it was just one of those click-bait stories that were all gossip and no substance. The sheep had clearly ended up as someone's Sunday roast. It was blatant poaching.

Nevertheless, he called Barney closer to him. Eyes darting all around. Ears on full alert.

He could have turned round and walked back. He certainly had the urge to follow his gut instinct, but he was also a stubborn man. He wasn't going to get spooked by an imaginary spectre. If he'd come to the woods to walk, then he was going to do just that.

The roar of the wind in the treetops blocked out the other sounds of the forest – including that of any unwelcome companions. Spring was still only a daffodil tip through the earth and the late winter sun's rays struggled to burn through the clouds, let alone penetrate the thick forest canopy, creating pockets of darkness.

The recent rain had reinvigorated the smells of the forest: pine, damp leaf mulch, the occasional waft of fox scent. Justin's nose wasn't anywhere near as effective as his dog's, but still the woodland filled his nostrils with its heady aroma.

He made up his mind to walk to the clearing with the ancient yew and then turn back for home. Barney knew the route and he ran on ahead, nose to the ground, tail wagging. As they walked and the black spectre hadn't reappeared, Justin began to relax. He'd complete his circuit and then head home for a decent cup of tea and maybe one of the hot cross buns his wife had bought that morning. Then he might do a bit of clearing up in the garden, clear the weeds from between the patio stones.

They were almost at the clearing.

In front, the sound of Barney barking brought his attention back and made his heart lurch. It wasn't the excited bark of a rabbit hunt; it was the bark of something that Barney didn't like. He had run out of sight and so Justin called him, trying to bring him to heel.

Justin hesitated, coming to a standstill and looking around nervously, waiting for his dog. He scanned 360 degrees, eyes flicking to the gaps between trees, searching for movement. His ears strained to hear any other sounds: the crack of breaking twigs underfoot, a voice, footsteps. There was nothing. Nothing but endless trees, the wind, and his dog.

Barney didn't reappear, and his barking continued. Taking a

deep breath and telling himself to 'man up', Justin walked forward and into the clearing ready to admonish his disobedient dog.

Barney was standing in the middle, four paws firmly planted, his hackles up. But Justin didn't look at his dog. Instead, his attention had been immediately seized by the reason for Barney's discomfort. Justin gasped aloud in shock. In front of them, hanging from the ancient yew tree, was a half-naked man with a wooden spear impaled through his middle. Blood dripped down his white skin and lettering had been carved onto his bare chest. The sight and smell of iron-laden blood turned Justin's stomach, and his breathing became instantly shallow and rapid. But, it was the man's eyes that froze his heart. They stared in front of him. Empty. Unseeing.

2

It wasn't that Dr Harrison Lane was bored. He'd been having a wonderful time with his girlfriend, Tanya, at the luxury hotel, but after two days and nights of doing essentially nothing, it had taken every ounce of his willpower not to break his promise and turn his mobile phone back on. A lifetime of being a workaholic was not easily erased in one short holiday.

The long weekend away had been his Christmas present to her after countless cases up and down the country had kept them apart. He'd left his Ritualistic Behavioural Crime Unit in the very capable hands of his assistant, Ryan, and Harrison and Tanya had ridden off on his Harley Davidson bike for their quality time together.

Spending time doing nothing had also allowed him to occasionally brood on the circumstances which had led him into this career. On his mother's murder all those years ago, and who had killed her. Last year he'd thought he was making progress, but catching up with Desmond Manning and being able to finally get some answers from him before he was put behind bars, had served only to show him that Desmond was the lowlife weasel he'd always thought he was; and that it wasn't Desmond, but somebody far more powerful behind her murder. Somebody with influence and ears in the police force itself. While Harrison relaxed with Tanya, he knew it could only be a temporary break from the hunt that had consumed him since he was eighteen.

Part of his gift to Tanya, was for her to spend a day in the spa, getting a few treatments and being pampered. She'd asked if he wanted to join her but it wasn't his idea of relaxing. He was an outdoor person and being cooped up inside a humid spa with a bunch of strangers was not his idea of fun. He'd sighed in relief when Tanya said she didn't mind. It would enable him to go for a run on his own – to exorcise the demons which were growing inside of him, making his muscles twitch with frustration.

'But what will you do? I can't leave you on your own,' Tanya said.

Harrison looked down into her blue eyes and tucked a strand of brunette hair behind her ear.

'Seriously, I'd like you to enjoy yourself. This is your present. Besides, now that the rain's stopped, I'd like to go for a run. Have a massage and a facial, chill out in the spa, and I'll meet up with the newly relaxed you for dinner later.'

Being together wasn't hard, it was surprisingly very pleasant. They'd been seeing each other for almost a year now, despite Harrison's initial fears that being in a relationship might ruin his concentration and distract him from his work. The ease with which they got on was partly helped by Tanya understanding his job. As a senior forensics officer, she knew what was involved in investigating major crimes. More than that though, she understood what drove him: his need to stop those who try to use religion and peoples' beliefs to hurt others. He did worry that his preoccupation with helping victims might mean Tanya didn't get the attention she deserved and at times he questioned if he was being fair to her. Would she be better off with someone else? That was a question too big to answer in one afternoon and so instead he'd got his bag out, ready to find his running gear and get changed.

Underneath the T-shirt, in the bottom of his bag, was his mobile phone, the screen black and cold. For a few moments he'd stared at it, his fingers itching to reach out and pick it up. He was a man of iron will. His levels of concentration and focus could rival any chess grand master, but the truth was, he wanted to turn it back on. He'd been expecting a phone call before he went away and it was one he desperately wanted to take.

The sight of the screen coming back to life felt like an intravenous adrenaline drip to his system. His brain started buzzing again and a wave of anticipation flowed through him.

He had four missed calls. One from Ryan, two from Detective Inspector Seb Bartholomew at the National Crime Agency, and the one he'd been hoping for – from Inspector Rob Morgan.

Inspector Morgan had been one of the police officers who'd attended his mother's so-called suicide almost twenty years ago. At the time he'd been a new recruit, but neither he nor his more experienced partner had believed she'd committed suicide. They believed that she'd been murdered. However, their chief superintendent had overruled them and there'd been nothing he'd been able to do about it. Harrison had been grateful for Morgan's honesty at the meeting they'd had in London last year, but now he had more questions for the inspector and was hoping they could meet up again.

At the sight of the missed call from Inspector Morgan, Harrison's stomach fizzed and he eagerly reacted to the next alert, that someone had left a message. He hoped it would be Rob's voice he heard and he wasn't disappointed.

Hi, Harrison, yes, sure, happy to meet up. Don't think I'll be able to make it to London, but happy to chat. Give me a call when you get this and we can fix a time. I'll look into that specific query you had. See if I can find out before we talk.

This was exactly what Harrison had been hoping for. Since

they'd spoken last, Harrison had discovered a lot more about the circumstances around his mother's death and so he had new questions for Rob. The message had been left the day before yesterday and so he called him straight back.

'Rob, it's Harrison, thanks for coming back to me. Will you have any time to talk later this week?'

There were a few moments of silence on the other end of the phone.

'Rob? Inspector Morgan?'

'Yes. Sorry, Harrison. Look, I'm really sorry but I'm flat out here. Going to have to delay our meeting. There's nothing much I can tell you anyway, I'm afraid. I think it's probably best left alone.'

It took Harrison three seconds to realise that something was up. Rob was sounding nervous. His throat constricted, making the tone of his voice rise.

'Is everything OK, Rob?'

'Yeah, yeah, all fine. Sorry, I can't talk right now. I'll call you when I can. OK?'

The line went dead.

There was no doubt that something very definitely wasn't all fine. His first thought was that Rob might be in a dangerous situation.

Harrison called Ryan.

'Boss! Thought you were on enforced radio silence, everything OK?' Ryan's cheerful voice nearly brought a smile to Harrison's face.

'Yeah, all good. Tanya's in the spa. I need you to do something for me. Inspector Rob Morgan of Gloucestershire constabulary, could you call and find out if he's OK? I've just had a weird phone call with him and it's for one of two reasons. Either he's in a dangerous situation and can't talk, or he just doesn't want to talk to me.'

'No worries. I'll do it now.'

Harrison paced up and down the hotel room while he waited for Ryan to ring him back. He knew his assistant would be inventive and come up with some excuse as to what he wanted. It took less than five minutes.

'Boss, he's fine. I called, said I'd lost my cat. He very patiently told me what I should do and seemed absolutely fine.' Ryan chuckled.

'OK. Thanks. That's good. I'm glad he's OK.' Harrison's mind wandered to why it would be that Rob had changed his mind about helping him. The answer was probably a simple one – he'd been warned off. The next question he would have to answer was, how had they found out?

'You know Seb at the NCA has been looking for you?' Ryan broke into his thoughts. 'Boss? You still there?'

'Yeah, sorry, Ryan.'

'He kind of wanted you urgently, says there's a new investigation they want you to help on, but I told him you were unlikely to be available until end of tomorrow earliest.'

'What is it?'

'Some bloke has been found hanging in a forest with strange symbols carved into his chest. It's literally just an hour's drive from where you're staying so not sure if you can swing over there on your way home tomorrow?'

'OK, I'll speak to DI Bartholomew,' Harrison said to Ryan, sighing.

His worries about what was going on with Rob Morgan would have to wait.

'Harrison, I thought you were still on holiday?' Seb Bartholomew answered his call.

'I am, but I've got a few hours spare.'

'Have to say I'm impressed with Ryan's loyalty. No amount of bribery or torture would get your current location out of that man.'

Harrison felt a warm glow of pride.

'I understand that the crime is not that far from me.'

'Oh, really? Then that's a real result. It's only been called through to us in the last hour or so and they've requested specialist help. If you could go tomorrow morning that would no doubt be appreciated.'

'So the crime scene's still active?'

'Yes, absolutely. Forensics were still working as the detective inspector in charge was speaking to me.'

'OK. Send me the details and I'll head over there now.'

'Now? Really? Are you sure? I didn't want to interrupt your holiday.'

'Absolutely. I'll get far more out of viewing a fresh crime scene than reading a report on it tomorrow morning.'

'I'll call him now and let them know you're on your way,' Seb replied.

Harrison shoved his running kit back into his bag and zipped it up. Then, he wrote a note for Tanya in case she returned early from the spa, saying, *See you at dinner*, and headed out to his Harley.

3

The location of the crime scene was in a forest on the Surrey and West Sussex borders. Harrison arrived at a public car park on the edge of the woods, which had been closed to all except the emergency personnel. The young, uniformed officer on duty was expecting him.

'I'll let the DI know you're here. Bit of a walk, I'm afraid. Up through them trees and keep going straight.' The officer pointed to a gap in the tree line, which thankfully clarified his directions – everywhere Harrison looked, there were trees.

After forty-eight hours confined inside thanks to the rain, Harrison craved the fresh air and a walk through the woods. He pushed the thought of what he was going to find at the end out of his mind. That was not going to be so pleasant.

For now, Harrison let the life and history of these ancient woodlands envelop him. An information board at the start of the path told him that the forest had been planted centuries ago, and both native deciduous and evergreen trees had grown there. The oak, birch, and beech trees were still in winter mode, bare brown branches with the odd dried leaf clinging on before a final death spiral to the forest floor. On some, he could just see the first buds of spring leaves breaking out like freckles in the sun.

The path he walked along was well worn and although he looked all around him, there was no point in trying to use the tracking skills he'd learnt as a child here. Walkers, dogs, horse riders, and most recently, the investigation team, had all walked ahead of him so the path was a smorgasbord of signs with no way of knowing which, if any, belonged to the killer. Harrison wasn't sure of the scale of the woods, but there were probably other potential easy access points for the killer to have entered and left. He knew that the investigation team would want to remove the body soon for the dignity of the victim and to ensure no voyeurs or press photographers were able to reach the scene from any number of directions. Maintaining a tight closed cordon in these circumstances would be difficult.

When he'd been walking for around ten minutes, he saw a figure coming along the path towards him. A young woman, dressed smartly – so not a walker, but more likely a detective. He suspected this might be his welcoming committee.

'Dr Lane?' The young woman enquired, appraising his tall, muscular frame. Harrison could see that she had been expecting somebody a little different.

'Yes.'

'I'm Detective Constable Sally Gorman. Detective Inspector Tony Painter asked me to escort you to the crime scene.'

Harrison estimated that Sally was in her mid-twenties and in the early stages of her career where the reality of the job was just beginning to dawn on her. Another month of sitting mostly working phones and doing paperwork might have killed all enthusiasm for why she'd joined up in the first place. This murder must have seemed like everything she'd become a detective for.

DC Gorman had short brown hair, cut in a sensible bob, and her clothes looked relatively new. Harrison guessed that she'd probably bought them with her first pay, determined to look the part in her new career. The ambition shone from her – and he couldn't miss the eagerness in her eyes.

DC Gorman turned and walked back with him. He could feel her bubbling by his side. His lack of conversation was too painful for her – and like so many before her, she had to fill the void.

'Tell the truth, I was glad to get away. It's really creepy in that clearing. It's like some kind of sacrifice, they've—'

'I'd be grateful if you would not give me any opinions or preliminary findings about the crime scene,' Harrison interrupted her. 'I prefer to work with a totally fresh eye and unbiased mind.'

'Oh!' was all she said, and a red flush rose up her cheeks.

Harrison realised he'd embarrassed her.

'The second that an idea is planted in our minds, it becomes a part of our own thinking and memories. It means we may not chase the more elusive perspectives but instead take the easy option of the already voiced view. It perpetuates bias and bandwagon thinking. It clouds what we ourselves see.'

There was a pause before she replied.

'Like the stuff we learnt in witness interviewing?' Sally's face returned to its previous bright-eyed enthusiasm. 'Witness memories can be easily contaminated by hearing other people's accounts of the same event.'

'Yes, or even leading questions can corrupt memories. I want to view the crime scene from a purely factual perspective, without any opinions which might push me to a different conclusion than one I might make alone.'

'Yeah, I get it.'

They walked on a little further in mutually comfortable silence, until further up the path, Harrison saw a uniformed officer and to the left and right, two others among the trees: the inner cordon to prevent any unwanted visitors.

Up to this point, the canopy of trees had kept the light muted. There were enough tall evergreens to compensate for the skeletal deciduous trees as barriers to the weak sun. As Harrison and Sally stepped past the police officer and into the clearing, the sky opened up above, illuminating the terrible scene in front of them.

Immediately, a tall, well-built man with a receding hairline looked up from what he was doing.

'Dr Lane! About time. We need to get this fellow down but were told to wait for your arrival.'

'That's DI Painter,' Sally said quietly to Harrison.

He assessed the situation. The DI was in his late fifties, almost certainly about to hit retirement age. He presumed that Seb Bartholomew had instructed the DI to wait for his arrival, which clearly hadn't gone down too well.

'I won't take long. I just need to make an initial assessment,' Harrison said to him.

'We've been hanging around for ages,' laughed another, younger detective who sported a short beard and moustache.

Sally tutted beside Harrison.

'That's Detective Sergeant Freddie Reid. Prat,' she whispered to him.

'DI Painter, would you mind asking everyone to step aside for just a few minutes while I look at the crime scene? Then I promise you that you can get on,' Harrison said.

'Step aside? What, you mean like get out of the clearing?'

'Preferably, if you wouldn't mind.'

DI Painter puffed out his chest, adjusted his shoulders, and sniffed. 'Ten minutes. That's it,' he said, enjoying flexing his authority. 'We all have jobs to do.'

All the staff in the clearing, including the white-suited forensic team, had stopped to watch the exchange. Harrison could feel them all weighing him up.

'Me too?' Sally said at his side, hopeful.

'Please.'

'OK.'

Harrison waited patiently for everyone to leave and then stood still with his head bowed and eyes closed as he gathered his concentration. He focused on his breathing, drawing in the scent of rotting leaves and pine needles, filling his chest and emptying it again, blanking out the whispering voices behind him. He could hear the waves of wind in the treetops, and the tinkling of glass and clanking of bamboo wind chimes, which were hung around the old yew tree. These gave a constant accompaniment to the forest orchestra, adding a layer of sound that was neither quite human nor quite natural. A memory tried to surface from his childhood. Harrison shut it away and forced his mind to focus only on the here and now.

Then, he opened his eyes and looked at the reason for his being there.

He was a young man, probably early thirties, with a beard and long hair that was just past his shoulders. He'd been hung by the neck, suspended from the ancient yew tree. Sticking out of his stomach was a large wooden spear from which blood had been dripping. The emergency services team had clearly not needed to cut him down quickly to see if they could find signs of life. The man was very obviously dead. Harrison guessed that blood had started to pool, but he wore jeans and trainers, so they were saved the purple hue of his lower body.

Apart from the spear through his gut, he had symbols carved into his bare torso. Harrison recognised them immediately. From where he stood, he could also see a tattoo on the victim's left arm. It was the World Tree, Yggdrasil, a twisted trunk with its leaf-laden branches reaching down and connecting the universe with its three roots.

The rope which held him had been tied to one of the many branches of the yew. Harrison noted it was too tall for a human being to have reached up and secured it.

The symbolism of the whole scene was clear to Harrison.

There was nothing further he could glean from the victim until he'd been brought down and so Harrison turned his attention to the forest floor. The ground was soft after the recent rain and the forensic team had placed stepping plates over certain areas. They protected horse hoof prints and an area where it looked as though some kind of scuffle had taken place. Like the forensic team before him, Harrison surmised that was where the victim was attacked. A scuffed trail in the leaves and mud led to the yew where he'd obviously tried to resist being dragged to the tree. Harrison turned his attention to the pattern of horse hoof marks and studied them closely. They were inexorably merged with the victim's footprints so clearly not just from a rider who may have visited the clearing earlier: the man's attacker had been on horseback. That tallied with the height that the rope had been secured.

The yew was impressive, probably over a thousand years old. Its main trunk was split and hollowed, and younger trunks were growing up around it where the branches had bent down to the ground and rooted. No doubt this tree had attracted human rituals and prayers for generations. From ancient to modern times, trees had been worshipped as sacred. The yew held a particularly significant role. Thanks to its own evergreen state and regenerative ability, it was revered for being seemingly immortal and found where both pagans and Christians worshiped – and judging by the tattoo on the victim's arm, he may well have agreed with that practice. The wind chimes hanging from the yew's branches showed that others visited this place for some form of contemplation or worship. Harrison could imagine that in different circumstances, the clearing and its magnificent tree would be cathartic.

Later, the forensic team would search the clearing for any potential evidence, but Harrison looked for himself. With his expert knowledge and tracking skills, there were often signs that might be missed by the detectives and forensics team who were looking for more standard evidence.

The circle scraped into the debris of the forest floor was barely visible, and interrupted by the horse hoof imprints and scuffed by the police investigators, but it was there. He followed its circumference and saw the occasional splash of white wax where candles had overspilled. Some kind of ritual had taken place here, but the murder had happened afterwards. Was it a consequence or part of this ritual, or unconnected?

Harrison inspected the trunk of the yew. There were a couple of crudely carved initials, but these were most likely from young lovers who had walked to the clearing over the years and nothing of interest to him. He then walked around the area, looking at each tree individually. If this was a regular ritual site, then he might expect to see symbols carved into the bark of the trees. He found nothing.

Harrison pointed the circle and wax out to the forensics photographer stood at the edge of the clearing, so that it could be recorded as potential evidence. Now, it was time to give the victim some dignity and release him from the noose.

'Thank you,' Harrison said to Painter as he approached the DI and his two-strong team.

Without a word, the detective raised his arm and gestured for everyone to return to the clearing, like some old sheriff telling his posse to head on in.

'So, you're a specialist detective?' he asked Harrison.

'I'm not a police detective. I'm a psychologist with ritualistic crime as my specialism.'

'You're a shrink?'

'No. I'm a criminal psychologist. Not a psychiatrist or psychotherapist. I look at what has happened and try to determine why a perpetrator was motivated to act in a certain way. That way we can determine the type of person who committed the crime, and are more likely to apprehend them.'

'So?'

'So, I think I need a bit more to go on than just what we can see here. I'm pretty clear on the symbolism in his mode of death, but I'd like to know a bit more about the victim before I make any assumptions. Do we know who he is?'

'Yeah. He's a local tree hugger. Dax Moore. Runs forest bathing therapy according to his website. Load of old baloney if you ask me, but apparently middle-class idiots are happy to part with their cash.'

'Actually,' Harrison corrected, 'there's lots of research to show forest bathing is very good for reducing stress, depression, and enhancing sleep and health. Modern people spend too much time indoors. Even here in the UK, nature is being prescribed to help those suffering from mental illness and it's said to boost your immune function as the plant phytoncides increase the body's antimicrobial proteins.'

DI Painter had listened with a look of stunned indifference at the mini lecture.

'Yeah, well, I prefer my nice comfy sofa in my centrally heated home, to sitting out here in a cold damp forest.' He huffed.

'He looks like Christ hanging up there. Is that your symbolism?' Detective Sergeant Freddie Reid spoke up now. He had a cocky look on his face that suggested he thought he'd got it right.

'No,' Harrison replied. 'His beard and hair might give you that kind of impression, but it's nothing to do with Christianity. Some kind of ritual has also taken place here, which may or may not be connected.'

'Could that be the killer's initials carved on his chest, or someone they're getting revenge for? *M*, *F*, *P*. Have they left their calling card for us?' DI Painter asked.

'Unfortunately not,' Harrison replied. 'Those aren't the letters M, F, or P.'

'Are they runes?' Sally asked. 'I've seen symbols like them on the old Viking stone on the heath.'

'Yes.' Harrison smiled at her. 'They are indeed runes.'

She smiled to herself. Harrison didn't miss the daggered look from DS Reid.

'Well, let's go take a closer look,' DI Painter butted into her moment of glory. 'He's coming down now, and the pathologist is on site to give us an initial assessment.'

As they walked over to the yew and the small crowd gathered around the body of their victim, Harrison heard DS Reid whispering to Sally.

'What the hell's a rune?'

'What you got for us, Dr Bannister?' DI Painter asked a woman bending over Dax Moore.

'Apart from the obvious? Not a lot at the moment.' She looked up and clocked Harrison before returning to professional mode and her victim. 'He died by hanging – obviously – but, unfortunately for him, it was the slow asphyxiation type as the rope tightened round his throat, as opposed to a quick clean neck break.'

'What about the spear?'

'Yes, hard to miss that,' she replied wryly. 'That wasn't really life threatening, more dressing than murder weapon.'

Harrison looked closely at the spear itself, searching for any indications as to why that particular one had been used. What looked like a large arrow had been carved into the shaft.

'Was he speared before or after hanging?' DI Painter pushed.

'Let me get him on my table and I'll try to answer that question. And I know what you're going to ask next. Time of death. I'll need to determine night-time temperatures properly, take his core readings, and examine his lower body, but I would hazard it was sometime late yesterday afternoon or early evening.'

'Righto,' DI Painter said, sighing. 'Back to the incident room for us then, while Mr Moore here gets shipped out and forensics finish up.'

'He was obviously hanging around all night then!' DS Reid retried his earlier joke on the pathologist.

'Have some respect for the victim, would you?' Dr Bannister snapped back – and immediately went up several notches in Harrison's estimation.

'Whoa, just a light-hearted joke, doc,' Reid replied, holding his hands up in mock surrender.

She glared at him with disgust.

'Blimey. Must be someone's time of the month!' Reid muttered under his breath as he walked off.

'What did you just say?' Dr Bannister shouted after him. 'Did you make a derogatory comment related to my gender?'

Reid looked slightly panicked. He was clearly not used to being challenged and everyone was watching.

Dr Bannister was standing staring at him, not about to step down. 'Well?' she reiterated.

DS Reid looked as though he didn't know what to say.

Harrison frowned at him. 'The doctor is waiting,' he added calmly.

Reid ground his teeth and replied through a clenched jaw. 'Sorry, Doctor Bannister. I was merely making a light-hearted joke and hadn't meant to offend you – or the victim. I apologise.'

'I won't make a formal complaint this time,' Dr Bannister replied, 'but don't ever talk to me – or any other woman – like that again.'

She gave an almost imperceptible nod to Harrison and turned her back on Reid. Harrison could see it had upset as well as angered her and she didn't want to show DS Reid that he'd got to her.

'Told you he was a prat.' Sally appeared at Harrison's side as he headed down the path to the car park.

'Is he always like that?'

'He's got worse. DI Painter's retiring in a couple of months and he's after promotion.'

Harrison sighed. If he had a senior investigating officer who was retiring, that might mean he didn't have his eye on the ball – and if his second-in-command was the class idiot, it definitely didn't bode well. Harrison had hoped to be in and out of here quickly, but getting justice for the victims was his priority, and that might just mean the pressure on him had been increased.

4

The walk back to the car park was a silent one – and not because of Harrison's default style of communication. Everyone was processing the horrific scene in the clearing, thinking about the victim, and who might have done that to him. The light was beginning to fade, and a team passed them on their way into the forest with what looked to be a generator and some lights. Forensics would be there for a few more hours yet.

The presence of other people seemed to jolt Sally out of her silence.

'I think I'm going to have nightmares tonight,' she said to Harrison quietly. 'This is my first murder investigation.'

'It's never easy having to come face-to-face with the terrible things humans can do to each other, even when we're professionals,' Harrison replied, gently. He was impressed that she'd been brave enough to admit it.

'Yeah, that clearing just gave me the creeps.' She furrowed her forehead.

'Obviously our murder victim will be the main reason, but I don't think the wind chimes and the remote location helped either,' Harrison said to her. 'They probably impacted your psychobiological stress system. If you wore headphones with relaxing music playing, your cortisol levels – the stress hormone – would have been considerably reduced.'

'Why? Why would wind chimes make me more stressed?'

'Do you watch horror movies?' he asked her.

'Yeah,' she looked at him, eyes narrowed. 'What's that got to do with it?'

'Wind chimes are an often-used tactic in horror movies where their discordant sounds are used to create an eerie effect to build up suspense. Had you been a natural health practitioner, you might have had the opposite experience. Found them relaxing.'

Sally thought for a moment.

'It's my dodgy memory again,' she smiled. 'My interpretation of the situation being based on my experiences.'

'Exactly. And obviously all the visuals, the victim, the symbolism of the murder, and the almost mystical yew tree: they've combined with your subconscious to create the feeling.'

'Yeah. Yeah, you're right – and the stories of the wolfman who supposedly lives in these woods.'

Sally stopped and put her hand over her mouth. 'Sorry, was I not supposed to tell you that?'

'No, it's fine. I've assessed the crime scene now. The next stage is information gathering. You should tell me more about the local stories. I need to know as much as possible about the victim that you can provide, too.'

'I think he was one of those eco campaigners, you know, goes on protests and ties himself to things to stop cars and roads.'

'That could be important.'

'Yes. I think he's part of a group. We'll no doubt be talking to them straight away.'

By now, they had arrived back at the car park where DI Painter was waiting for them. Harrison needed to get back to the hotel in time to go for dinner with Tanya. She'd be finishing up at the spa about now and wondering where he was.

'We're heading to the incident room,' DI Painter said. 'Can you give us a briefing on this symbolism of yours?'

'I can give you a quick summary here, but I have to get back. My hotel is an hour away. I'll return tomorrow and give you a full briefing in the morning.'

'An hour away? There's plenty of hotels around here. Where are you staying?' DS Reid asked.

'Alexander House.'

'That's well posh, that is. They certainly look after you at the NCA.'

'It's not for work. I'm technically on leave at the moment. I came today because I wanted to see the crime scene fresh.'

'Well, we'll be working through the evening, so are there any insights you can give us? You said you recognised the symbolism.' DI Painter interrupted the accommodation discussion.

'Yes. This goes back to Vikings and Norse mythology. Their god, Odin, who ruled Valhalla, was said to have speared himself and hung from a tree, which they call Yggdrasil, or the World Tree, while searching for the secrets of life and death and the meaning of the runes. That tree was believed to be either an ash or a yew. Your victim was staged like Odin and he had runes carved into his torso. Ansuz, Thurisaz, and Ehwaz. His killer clearly has some knowledge of Viking and Norse mythology, but there's likely a deeper meaning here which may be found in the runes and in the mythology around the story and the life of the victim.'

'Bloody hell, so we've got a nutter running around who thinks he's a Viking?' DI Painter exclaimed.

'They don't necessarily think they're a Viking, but perhaps they have an affinity with Norse mythology and some kind of spiritual connection to the runes. So when you're thinking about potential suspects, look out for it.'

'And what exactly are these runes?'

'They're the ancient alphabet used by the Germanic nations, from which the Vikings came.'

'Always found history boring at school,' DS Reid muttered.

'We're all products of history, DS Reid. It has shaped our societies and our landscape, and determined our own genetic make-up. It cannot be ignored because it is a part of so many of our rituals and belief systems.'

DI Painter did his shoulder shrug and sniff. 'Well, we need to get back to the office to focus on some modern police work. Dr Lane, we'll see you tomorrow.'

DI Painter and DS Reid walked off to their car.

'Goodnight, Dr Lane,' Sally said to him, smiling, and followed her boss.

Harrison returned to his Harley and fired up the engine. He hoped that tomorrow morning would bring good news, that they'd have a strong suspect and he'd be able to get back to London with Tanya as planned. The conversation he'd had with Inspector Rob Morgan was twisting around his guts and sending warning signals to his brain.

5

As Harrison rode back to the hotel, the sound of his motorbike
engine silenced the tinkling and clanking of the wind chimes
which had been in his ears and mind since the forest. It took
him back to Wales and the commune where he and his mother
had lived with the Mannings. There had been wind chimes all
around the place, a constant backing track to their daily life. But
he didn't want their evil seeping into his mind, or the anger that
rose in his gut whenever he thought about his mother's murder.
He needed to focus on the murder in the here and now, and help
get it solved.

He'd already texted Ryan to ask him to get as much information as he could on Dax Moore and any organisations he might
belong to. It was unlikely that somebody had taken offence to
his forest bathing – the environmental activism was a far more
likely source of enemies and that was no doubt one of the areas
that DI Painter's team would be focusing on. The question was,
why had the killer staged him like that? And what role did
Viking mythology have in Dax's life or the life of his murderer?

Harrison pushed all these thoughts, past and present, away
with an image of a relaxed Tanya waiting for him back in their

hotel room. He avoided thinking about how he was going to explain to her where he'd been.

When he got back to their room, Tanya was in the shower.

'Hi, it's me,' he shouted through the door.

'Won't be long,' she returned.

Harrison took one last look at his phone and turned it off. He'd seen the crime scene, now he had to honour his promise to Tanya – even if it was a bit late.

Tanya exited the bathroom in a billow of steam. She had her hair up in a towel and another larger bath towel wrapped around her body.

'I was smothered in oil,' she said by way of explanation for her shower.

'Did you enjoy it?' Harrison asked, putting off the inevitable question about his afternoon.

'Yes, it was glorious. Thank you. My neck and shoulders haven't felt so supple in years.' She looked at him. 'So, what have you been up to this afternoon? Did you go for a run and a walk?'

Harrison realised she was looking at his clothing, which wasn't his running gear, and then down to his feet. He glanced at his shoes and saw the telltale smears of forest mud and mulch.

'You'd make a good forensic detective...' He smiled. 'I'm sorry. I know I promised, but there was a murder an hour away. They'd requested my help and if I left it until tomorrow then I'd have missed seeing the crime scene as it was.' He sighed and sat down on the bed to take his shoes off before he got mud on the carpet.

'So, was sending me off to the spa a ploy to get me out the way?'

'No. No, I promise that I had intended to just go for a run...' He tailed off.

'Well, if you want to work every day and send me to the spa

then I'm not going to argue,' Tanya teased. 'It's fine. Honestly. I've only been back half an hour and as long as you promise not to talk shop over dinner, then I'll still have had a lovely day. We've been glued to each other for two days. I get it.'

'Thank you,' Harrison said to her, and meant it.

'So, I presume you spoke to Ryan? How's his new flat working out? You're going to miss that wall of boxes when you get home.'

'I'm pretty sure I won't miss his boxes, but he was an easy house guest otherwise. He's doing fine. We were lucky to find his new place. Less likely to have neighbours who might spring bad surprises.' Harrison thought back to the urgent evacuation he'd had to arrange after Ryan had been recognised by a member of a gang he'd previously been forced to work for.

'That's good. You know, if you want to drop me at the train station tomorrow morning once we've checked out, I can make my own way back to London.'

Harrison studied her face and tone of voice for any signs that she was annoyed.

'Are you absolutely sure? I could take you home and then come back.'

'Don't be silly. As long as you promise to have a nice leisurely breakfast with me, it's fine. Anyway, if I'm honest, the way the weather's been these last few days, a nice warm train carriage sounds a lot more inviting than the back of a motorbike.'

'Only if you're sure,' Harrison said, standing up from the bed and walking over to her, putting his arms around her warm, semi-naked body.

She smiled up at him, their eyes connecting.

'We've got over an hour before dinner,' she said suggestively.

As her towel dropped to the bedroom carpet, Harrison realised how lucky he was that he had an understanding girl-friend who really didn't mind if he went AWOL investigating murder scenes.

. . .

Harrison honoured Tanya's request and didn't mention work again – and they had a very pleasant last evening together in the hotel. Instead, they'd talked about friends and Tanya's family, whether they both wanted to stay living in London, and what kind of dog they would each like to have. Tanya wanted a cockapoo – 'less hairs' she'd said to Harrison. Having lived with her parent's Labrador, she was also aware of the danger of energetic wagging tails. 'It's like having a toddler around, you have to Labrador-proof the house or you lose anything that's on low tables. Glasses of wine, mugs of tea, ornaments, they all just get swept off.'

Harrison had surprised her with his choice. 'I'd like a Jack Russell,' he'd said. 'They don't miss a thing which makes them great early warning systems, and they're fun and energetic but not so big you can't take them everywhere.'

'I thought you'd have been more of a big dog man,' Tanya had said to him.

'They're big dogs in small bodies. I haven't met a Jack Russell yet that thinks it's a small dog. I like that about them.'

Then they'd laughed about the names they might call their pooches, but stopped just short of combining their dogs into one household. That was something which Harrison hadn't yet dared to contemplate.

After dinner they relaxed in the sitting room area, Tanya drinking the rest of her red wine, and Harrison a chamomile tea. Two guests came over to say hello to them, a young couple in their late twenties, both lawyers from London. Tanya had met the woman, Juliette, in the spa and she and her boyfriend came and sat down on the sofa opposite them as though they were long-lost friends. Juliette proceeded to monopolise Tanya, chatting about her Oskia bamboo massage. Harrison was forced to listen to the boyfriend, Arthur, who decided to tell him far more information about them than Harrison needed to know. Perhaps it had been the wine with their food, or maybe they were just trusting souls, but within just a few minutes, Harrison knew which firm they worked for, and that they weren't supposed to have in-house relations, so that was why they'd come away from London for the weekend. He was also told where they lived in London, that his father had cancer but was being stoic about it, and that Juliette's parents lived on the Isle of Man.

What Arthur didn't tell him, was that he was stressed about his relationship with Juliette, no doubt worried that work would find out and as they were both in their first jobs after qualifying, it was a big concern. He also didn't say just how much his father's illness was upsetting him. These details Harrison gleaned from his voice, face, and body language, as well as the words he chose.

'You will enjoy each other's company far more if one of you looks for another job,' Harrison said to him.

'Yes, well, we've managed for the past year, but I must say it's becoming a strain. It's hard, isn't it, not to give it away with the way you talk to someone or look at them? Question is, which one of us should move?'

Harrison had looked over to Tanya and thought about how they'd first got together. She looked up and caught his gaze, smiling back. Arthur was right, if you care about someone it shows.

'Indeed,' he'd replied. 'Perhaps if it was you who changed jobs, you might be able to get a few weeks off and then be able to spend some time with your father?'

Harrison watched as that thought settled into Arthur's mind and a smile lightened his face.

'That is such a good call. Really hadn't thought about it that way. It's so damned difficult getting any time off; they work us hard and my folks live up in Yorkshire so it's not easy getting time with him. Would be good to go fishing again like we used to.'

Harrison could almost see the weight lifting off Arthur's shoulders and he was glad that perhaps he'd been able to help. Sometimes it just took a neutral third party to see the obvious and with just a few words, make a big difference.

If Harrison had been staying here alone, he wouldn't have sat in the sitting room area, open to social interactions. He would have kept himself to himself and most likely gone up to his room the minute he'd finished eating. Tanya enjoyed socialising, chatting to others as well as to him. He wondered if he would end up holding her back, cutting her wing feathers with his own reserve. That was not something he wished to do. Or would she ensure he was more sociable and help him break down some of his barriers?

Once Juliette and Arthur had gone, and Tanya disappeared to visit the toilet, Harrison sat and looked at the other people in the sitting room. Some were drinking and laughing, others quietly talking. You could tell those in the flush of new love compared to those who had been together a long time. The latter felt no need to talk. They were comfortable in their joint skin. There was an older couple just across the room to him. He'd seen them earlier, taking life slowly, and not hooked on the constant digital culture like some of the others who would stop for a selfie or to take a photograph of something that might look good on Instagram. He wondered if that could be him and Tanya in a couple of decades.

Would he be able to come away to a hotel and not feel the constant hunger for justice which throbbed away inside him? A reminder that he'd never be at peace. Even if he caught his mother's killer, there would always be another victim who'd need his help.

* * *

The next morning, Harrison and Tanya enjoyed a full cooked breakfast together, before he took her to the station just in time for the 9 a.m. to London. As Harrison waved her off, he felt both a sadness and excitement. It had been like living another life the past few days. Cocooned away from the world, totally immersed in each other and completely out of normal routine. It was time to get straight back into reality and face the terrible things that people do to each other. He had a job to do. A killer to help catch. A victim who needed justice. It was time for work.

6

Harrison arrived in the incident room midway through the morning briefing. DI Painter saw him slip in and stand at the back. There were about fifteen officers in the room, a mix of detectives, uniformed, and civilian support staff. One of the uniformed officers was explaining the geography of the crime scene to the room. Harrison listened in.

'The woods are mostly owned or managed by the Forestry Commission, which allows the public to access around half of the forest. There is an area that's out of bounds due to tree felling and the like. The clearing where our murder occurred is around thirty minutes' walk into the woods from the car park. It's a well-known spot that does get its fair share of walkers, but more usually on weekends. The dog walker who discovered the victim is retired and walks fairly regularly in the forest. Once in the clearing, you're about half an hour away from the nearest road, which is the car park end. There is an area of around fifteen acres on the eastern boundary, which is privately owned by the Holmes family. That backs onto their farm and is about forty minutes' walk from the clearing.'

'So, presuming there were no walkers in the woods at the

time, nobody would have heard our victim's screams or cries for help,' DI Painter summed up the situation.

'No,' the constable replied and went to sit down again.

'I'd like to introduce you all to Dr Harrison Lane at the back there. Dr Lane, do come forward.'

All heads swivelled to the back of the room, where Harrison was quietly watching from a corner. Reluctantly, he stepped forward as requested.

'Dr Lane is from the National Crime Agency and runs the Ritualistic Behavioural Crime unit. He's here to help us with the symbols on the victim's chest, and indeed the manner of his death. Some of you may have seen him yesterday because he visited the crime scene for us. As I explained earlier, Dr Lane has a theory that it's been staged like a mythical Viking god. Dr Lane, would you be able to give us any other thoughts and explain what the symbols are on Dax Moore's chest?'

DI Painter clearly didn't expect Harrison to say no, because he changed the images on the big screen, losing the aerial photograph of the woods and bringing up a close-up of the symbols carved onto Dax's torso.

'It's still too early for me to give you a full profile of the killer, but it's significant that they've used the Viking symbolism in the murder. When talking to suspects and acquaintances of the victim, look for an interest in the runes and Viking mythology. Like many cultures before and after them, the Vikings thought certain trees were sacred and worshipped them. This passion for trees clearly ties in with Dax's lifestyle, so it's also possible that somebody used his own beliefs against him: that the murderer is not actually interested in Vikings and runes at all, but has parodied them to further humiliate Dax. Either way, they clearly have more Norse mythology knowledge than you'd expect in the general population.'

'So, what do these symbols mean?' DI Painter asked.

'These three symbols are called Ansuz, Thurisaz, and Ehwaz.

Ansuz, the one that almost looks like a capital F with sloping arms, can represent a message. It refers to Odin and his wisdom, and often means communication, advice, truth; although it could mean the opposite, deceit and misunderstandings. Thurisaz is this one which looks like a large triangular flag mid-mast, about halfway down on a pole. It deals with chaotic forces, violence, betrayal, danger, a reactive force. Finally Ehwaz, the one which looks like a capital M, comes from the word yew, and it literally means horse. Some view it as the death card, but it's about transformation and renewal, as with the yew – a symbol of eternal life. All these three symbols can be linked to the murder.

'Looking at the horse hoof prints and the other evidence in the clearing, the killer was on horseback. He's hung him on a yew like Odin, and violence has been used. However, there are many more subtle messages in these symbols which we might not yet see. The important point to remember with the runes is that their meanings are not clear cut. They were used as an alphabet, but the Vikings also sought advice from the runes, casting them, and asking questions. When you read what has been cast, it relates to your individual questions and so one man's interpretation could be totally different to another's. I need to get to know the victim better.'

'Well, Dr Lane, you'll be pleased to hear that we've already identified a potential suspect: Chester Holmes. A member of the public had called in an argument involving him and Dax Moore two days previously. The lady had recognised Dax but not Chester and was concerned because she said it appeared to be quite a big row that was on the verge of turning violent. When officers arrived, they'd both dispersed, but the incident was logged and following his murder we were able to get CCTV footage of the dispute and identify Chester, who, by the way, is a keen rider. We're going to have a chat with him later this morning at his farm. Perhaps you'd like to come along and quiz him about his Viking knowledge?'

'I'd be delighted to,' Harrison replied.

'Good, well everyone knows what they're to focus on today. We don't know yet if Dax was killed by someone who knew him, or a stranger, so we need to keep an open mind. Dax's lifestyle wasn't exactly conventional but that doesn't mean he knew his killer. Why was he in that clearing in the first place? It does look like the killer was on horseback, so I want every horse owner within a twenty-mile radius tracked down. Are there any Viking groups around here? Check out every eco protest that Dax has been on. Has he messed with the wrong people?'

With that, DI Painter wrapped up the briefing, and the room erupted into a noisy hubbub. Sally appeared at Harrison's side.

'Morning, Dr Lane.' She smiled up at him. 'I know it might not be possible, but when it is, would you allow me to observe any interview techniques? I'd really like to improve on mine.'

'Of course. I'll keep that in mind.'

'Harrison, can I have a word?' DI Painter motioned for him to follow him to an office.

Once they were both inside, Tony Painter shut the door. He hesitated a moment before speaking, looking out the window with unfocused eyes. Harrison took this as a sign he was choosing his words carefully and hoped he wasn't about to try to debunk his theories. It wouldn't be the first time that a senior investigating officer refused to accept the variety and veracity of human belief systems. DI Painter looked old school.

'Look, I've no doubt you've been told that I'm retiring in less than three months, so I wanted to make something clear,' the DI started. 'I'm hoping this will be my last case, but I am not demob happy. I want to leave with a success. I intend to catch whoever strung that young man up, and I'd appreciate any help you can give us.'

Harrison looked into the determined face of the DI and gave an encouraging smile. It was good news, much better than he'd been expecting to hear.

'Absolutely. You have my help.'

'Good. I know DS Reid can be a bit of a prat at times and needs knocking into shape, but he's a good detective underneath all the bull. I've warned him that comments like he made yesterday will not be tolerated and I think he's taken it on board. It's DC Gorman's first murder case, but she's going to fast-track her way up the ladder with that keen mind. We've got a good team here. Just let me know what you need and I'll make sure you get it. Right now, we need to head out to see Chester Holmes. Find out if he could be our killer.'

Chester Holmes was what could be described as 'a person of interest'. He'd been seen arguing with the victim, and the family farm, which included a stable block, was on the edge of the woods. DI Painter and DS Reid, accompanied by Harrison, had arranged to meet Chester at his home to ask him a few questions. The most pertinent being, did he have an alibi and why were they arguing?

'Dr Bannister has given us a revised time of death. We're looking at between five p.m. and ten p.m. I'm guessing that the earlier time is more likely, as riding through the forest on a horse in the dark must be pretty dodgy,' DI Painter told Harrison in the car on the way there.

'I didn't see the cloud cover night before last. Was it extensive?' Harrison asked.

'Yes. Been bad all week.'

'Chester Holmes runs the family cupcake business. Does a roaring trade by all accounts. I think the father still runs the farm, but the cakes are the money spinner. They nearly went bankrupt a few years back.'

'Quite amazing really, considering he was a right loser at school. Was always getting detentions and I don't think he ever paid any attention in the cooking lessons,' Freddie added.

'Always had him down as an entitled arse, but the cupcakes were a stroke of genius. They're good, too. Doubt he's going to feel like letting us taste some, though, after we've asked him a few questions.'

They followed the tree line for a mile, before turning off at a pair of stone gates which carried an old sign for *Bemford Farm* and a new modern one saying *Bemford Cupcakes*. They drove for around four hundred metres, along a newly tarmacked drive.

'They've certainly been improving things,' DI Painter noted.

Towards the trees, a light industrial unit with a *Bemford Cupcakes* sign on it sat closest to the woods. The trees were a dark backdrop, looking still and sombre after their activity yesterday. A farmhouse, which had again undergone some recent refurbishment, took centre stage. Harrison noted a stable block and outdoor sand school for the horses to the right, and a paddock area with short, neatly mown grass stretching off flat and even.

'Doesn't look like they do much in the way of farming here anymore,' Freddie said.

As they pulled up outside the farmhouse, the front door was opened by a grey-haired man in corduroy trousers and a shirt and V-neck jumper. He looked to be in his late fifties, perhaps slightly older. Still fairly trim, and Harrison guessed he'd be an eligible bachelor – if he weren't married. An elegant blonde woman of around the same age appeared behind him. She looked like the dutiful wife going out in front of the media to support her errant political husband after some scandal or another. They were both clearly being protective of their son.

'Mr Holmes?' DI Painter approached them, hand extended.

'Phillip Holmes, and this is my wife, Dawn. Before you come into our home, we want to know what this is all about and if Chester should have a lawyer present?' Phillip crossed his arms over his chest and planted both feet firmly on the ground as though barring their entry.

'You are perfectly at liberty to instruct legal representation for your son, Mr Holmes, but we are just making enquiries at this stage, asking anyone who knew Mr Moore about their relationship with him.'

'Relationship? There was no relationship,' Dawn Holmes indignantly corrected the DI.

'They were seen arguing, Mrs Holmes. We need to enquire as to what the nature of that argument was.'

Harrison studied the Holmes's body language. Phillip looked in control and was clearly irritated by their presence. Dawn was a little nervy and obviously defensive of her son, a natural motherly reaction.

'You can come in, but if we detect any kind of attempt to drag our son's name into this, then I will be asking you to leave and calling a solicitor. Is that clear?'

'That's quite clear, Mr Holmes. I apologise, but I understood that your son was an adult in his twenties. Am I mistaken?'

Harrison knew that Painter was saying that purposely, pointing out that Chester should be able to speak for himself. He'd seen the detective's jaw muscle clench and unclench as Philip had spoken to him. He suspected the man was marking off the days on his calendar when he didn't need to put up with any more rudeness.

Phillip Holmes simply glared at Painter and turned around without another word. His wife dutifully followed him, and they all trooped into the house.

Chester Holmes was standing with his back to them in the sitting room, looking through the patio window doors to the woods beyond. When he turned at their arrival, his face was a picture of chilled innocence.

'Good morning, detectives. Freddie.' He nodded to DS Reid. 'I was very sorry to hear the news about Dax Moore earlier and

I'd be more than happy to help you with any enquiries, but I really didn't know the man well, so I hope this won't be a wasted trip for you.'

He was of average height, around five feet ten or eleven, but clearly worked out. There was also a surety about him which often came with the territory of money, and Chester's youth seemed to give him an added air of conceit.

'Thank you for agreeing to see us, Mr Holmes.' DI Painter didn't wait to be told to sit down. He settled himself onto one of the sofas, and DS Reid promptly parked himself next to him. Harrison stayed standing. Chester was the last of his family to choose a chair.

'So, fire away, detectives,' he said to DI Painter. 'And please, all take a seat.' The latter remark was aimed at Harrison, who had waited to see where everyone was going to sit down. Chester had chosen the chair facing the doorway, which, had they been sitting around a boardroom table, would have been at the head. It was a clue to the family dynamic.

'You said you didn't really know Dax Moore, but we have a witness who said they saw you arguing with Mr Moore two days ago in the centre of town.'

'That's correct,' Chester replied, 'but I can assure you it wasn't anything untoward. Dax runs some eco wellness busi-ness. I think he calls it forest bathing. I call it going for a walk in the woods. Anyway, he wanted me to invest in it. I declined. Simple. I've no idea why he thought I'd be interested.'

'If you didn't know each other, why did he approach you?'

'I know a couple of the others in his little tree hugging group. Summer Frances works as a groom for us. I'm guessing she suggested me.' Dax looked at his father.

'Anyone else?' DI Painter asked.

Chester looked quizzical, as though he had lost the train of conversation.

'You said you knew a couple of the others.'

'Ah yes, I think that Sam Green knows him. He's one of our cupcake delivery drivers. It could have been him, I suppose.' Chester shrugged.

'And you're not a part of their eco group?' Painter challenged.

'Absolutely not,' he replied indignantly. 'They're a nuisance. Get themselves arrested and keep blocking the roads so innocent motorists can't go about their business.'

DI Painter accepted his reply without further comment. 'I have to ask you where you were between the hours of five p.m. and ten p.m. the night before last?'

'I was here. My father and I had a business meeting. We're thinking about expanding the cupcake distribution with another facility.'

'I see.' DI Painter looked to Phillip Holmes, who was focusing on his son.

'That's correct,' Phillip said, realising that the detective was looking at him.

'You weren't perhaps out riding? Can anyone else corroborate that?'

Chester's face changed from benign friendliness to a hard stare.

'Are you saying you don't believe me?'

'I was asking if anyone else could confirm that.'

'I think, detective, that both of our words should be more than enough for you.' Phillip spoke again with authority in his voice. 'If you're looking for a killer, then I'd suggest you do a proper search of those woods. I've seen a man. He must be living rough out there somewhere. And I'm not the only one who's seen him. I don't think he's a wolfman like some of them are saying, but he has killed a sheep, so who's saying he wouldn't kill a man?'

'You've seen an individual in the woods?' DI Painter asked. 'When was this, and can you describe him?'

'Yes. He had shoulder length black hair and a beard. Thin

and not overly tall, I don't know, possibly about five six, or seven. I've seen him a few times, flitting about between the trees or peering out at us here.'

'The woods around the farm are private.' Chester took over from his father. 'We don't allow the public any access because of security concerns. They start wandering all over the place if you give them half an inch, and we have a business here. A food business that needs the highest hygiene standards.'

'I see. When was the last time you saw him?' DI Painter asked Phillip.

'A few days ago. I think Thursday, maybe.'

'OK, we'll look into it.' DI Painter jotted into the notebook that he held. 'Can I ask how many horses you have in the stables?'

'Four. I'm learning to play polo and have two ponies for that, plus we have two horses for hacking,' Chester replied.

'Polo? That's an expensive sport to play.'

'Yes, it is. I'm going to sponsor my own team and own a full string of ponies in the near future, but for now, I'm enjoying learning.'

'And were any of the horses taken out yesterday, late afternoon into early evening?'

'No. Summer and I exercised them earlier in the day.'

'Could anybody have taken one of the horses out without you knowing?'

'Absolutely not. I was down there yesterday morning and there was no sign that any horse had been out without permission.'

'I think we'd notice, detective, if somebody arrived at the stables and took one of our horses,' his father added.

'Do you have CCTV?'

'Not for the stables, no. We do around the cupcake unit,' Chester replied.

'OK. Please could you ensure that footage is retained in case we might need it?' DI Painter paused a few moments, thinking.

'Do you know anyone who is into Vikings? Perhaps consults with runes?' he asked, glancing at Harrison for reassurance that he'd said the right thing.

'Vikings?' Chester chuckled and looked at his parents. It was a hollow attempt at a laugh, which Harrison saw through.

'No. I can't say that I do. No. Not at all.'

This was the first time that Harrison detected a definite lie. He'd suspected some dishonesty earlier on in the interview, but Chester was a confident individual on his home turf. With this answer, his body language leaked dishonesty. The laugh was out of place and definitely fake. A tool to give himself time to think of what to say. He had also over-emphasised his negative reply, which smacked of him trying to convince them, rather than simply replying to the question. Plus, there had been several rapid blinks, which could sometimes be a subconscious sign that someone was lying. That their brain was working overtime to ensure they didn't slip up.

'Like my father said, you might spend your time better trying to find that wild man out in the woods, rather than questioning me, detective. I really didn't know the victim, and I had no reason to want to harm him.' Chester pushed his chin forward and up, giving a clear signal that he had said pretty much all that he was going to.

As soon as they were out of earshot of the house and its occupants, DI Painter turned to Harrison.

'So, what did you think? A cool customer, wouldn't you say?'

'Yes. Confident, but I'm not completely convinced by him. Definitely lying about knowing someone who was interested in Vikings and runes.'

'I agree. I'm not sure either way. Maybe he's protecting someone.'

'Interesting that the father mentioned the wolfman,' Freddie spoke up. 'That description of a man in the trees was just like the one that the dog walker gave. He'd seen someone just before he came across the body.'

'Yes, but it was a man on foot running in the opposite direction. Whoever killed Dax Moore was on horseback.'

'Could be a witness, then?' Freddie suggested.

'He could, so we're going to have to try and track him down. Get onto the dog team, would you? Find out when we can get them into the woods. We won't get sign-off on the helicopter without further evidence that he's going to help the inquiry, but we may get a heat-seeking drone if we're lucky.'

'I'll get on it,' Freddie replied.

As they reached the car, a waft of cake aroma reached them.

'That smells delicious. I could just sink my teeth into one of those cupcakes right now,' Freddie said, closing his eyes and breathing in deeply. 'Maybe it's the smell that's attracting our wolfman. If you're living rough in the woods, then that's going to be pretty tempting when you're hungry.'

'You might be right, Freddie,' DI Painter replied.

They all looked towards the dark band of trees that ran along the back of the farm, as though expecting to see a face peering out.

7

The face that looked out at the three men wasn't from the woods. To the side of a window in the farmhouse, the person stood, watching them leave.

The detectives' presence was incredibly irritating; now, they were going to have to do some clearing up. Ensure nothing could be found – just in case. They had too much to lose now to allow anyone to endanger it. They'd worked too hard and put everything on the line.

Things had got more complicated since that girl became involved. She'd created a weak point. The others couldn't see it yet, but they would.

8

───────

Instead of heading straight back to the station, DI Painter suggested they drive to Dax Moore's home. 'Forensics have just called. They've finished doing a sweep but said there's nothing unusual there. Let's see if we can get to know our victim a bit better. This will probably be particularly useful for you, Dr Lane.'

'Indeed, and Harrison, please,' he'd replied.

'It's less than ten minutes from here anyway,' Freddie added encouragingly.

Harrison had noticed a definite change in tone from the younger detective today. Whatever DI Painter had said to him yesterday, seemed to have worked.

* * *

Dax Moore's home was the polar opposite of the newly refurbished family farmhouse that they'd just left. A bumpy track led to a field and four static caravans in various states of repair and covered in green lichen. The only other structure in the field was a small brick outbuilding. The caravans were placed on pitches that had at one point been gravelled, but nature had reclaimed the area as its own and all that could be seen was the odd patch of shingle in the grass. There were clear signs that at least one of the caravans was lived in. There was a little BBQ area with some old wooden garden chairs in a circle around it next to the cleanest van, and discarded beer cans and bottles evidenced recent activity. All of this was set against the backdrop of the forest, a dark green wall of nature which rose up and filled the horizon. Here, Dax had been just a field away from his beloved trees.

'This all belongs to Wilson Johnson. He's a real character. Lives in the old cottage just over the hedge there. He's been told countless times that he shouldn't be renting these caravans out all year round as permanent dwellings, but the old bugger always manages to wriggle out of it. This used to be licensed as a campsite, back in the days when Wilson's wife was still around. Got some run-down shower and toilet facilities and that's about it. No tourist would fancy staying here, so now he tends to rent them to migrant workers and those living on low incomes,' DI Painter explained as they sat parked up by the entrance of the field. 'Dax's is the blue one.'

'Oi! What do you think you're doing?' A gruff voice came from outside the car, along with a sharp rap on the side window. All three turned at once to see a man in his sixties with long grey hair and a beard, brandishing a wooden walking stick.

'Bloody hell, it's Gandalf,' Freddie muttered to them.

'Mr Johnson, Detective Inspector Tony Painter, we've met before.' Tony turned off the engine and got out, walking towards their host with his hand outstretched.

'Your lot have already been round.' Wilson waved away Tony's hand. 'What do you want now?'

'We're investigating Dax's murder, and it's essential that we get to know him and his life, social circles, etc., as much as possible. We're just going to take a look around his caravan. Forensics have been in.'

Wilson's gruffness reduced noticeably, and he nodded his head, clearly satisfied that they weren't there to charge him with illegal rentals again.

'Aye, OK. I'd like the lad's killer found. Not right what happened to him.'

'Mr Johnson.' Harrison stepped forward. 'I don't suppose you'd know if Dax had an interest in the Vikings or Norse mythology, would you?'

'Vikings?' Wilson frowned as he thought. 'He was into lots of New Age health stuff, meditation, and yoga and all that crap, but never heard mention of any Vikings. That friend of his, Summer, I think she's called, she's into a load of mumbo jumbo stuff. Tried to read my fortune for me one day. I can't be doing with all that. Pretty thing, though, went along with it just to keep her happy.'

'What did she use to tell your fortune?' Harrison asked.

'Use? Well, it weren't a crystal ball. It were some kind of little tile things. She told me to think about what was worrying me and then chucked them out on the floor. Shame she didn't predict what happened to Dax.'

'Thank you,' Harrison replied and glanced at DI Painter.

'And before you goes charging me with renting them vans out.' Wilson became animated again and spoke to all three of them. 'I don't. Don't charge a penny for 'em. Dax used to help around the place, that's all. No contracts, no rental. I'll miss him. He was a good lad.'

'I take it that whatever fortune telling Summer was doing is related to your runes?' DI Painter asked Harrison the second they were out of earshot of Wilson. He'd noticed the ritualistic psychologist's interest.

'It certainly sounds like it. Other more common options would have been palm reading or Tarot cards, but small stones or tiles are usually runes.'

'Right, well, this Summer needs to be our next visit then. That's the second time her name has come up.'

'And she rides horses,' Freddie added, eyebrows raised. 'She's the Holmes's groom.'

'Indeed. Could this be some kind of cult thing, Dr Lane?'

'I haven't come across Norse and Viking mythology as a cult in the sense of what I think you're meaning. It's more about paganism and more recently the Ásatrú religion, not like the modern cults we see today which are usually led by one individual and are about mind control. Norsemen were free spirits. Of course, that's not to say it can't happen.'

'Good to know. Right, gloves on, just in case we find anything in here. Forensics have been in, but let's play on the safe side.'

They'd reached Dax's caravan. The aqua-blue paint had been partially washed down, and where the washing hadn't reached, towards the roof, green lichen and moss still populated. It looked as though someone had tried to create a pond effect. Unlike the dirty grey net curtains in the other vans, just fabric curtains were pulled back at the windows. It indicated that Dax wasn't paranoid about his privacy.

DI Painter was about to open the caravan door and go in when he looked behind him and saw that Harrison wasn't there.

'Where's he gone?' he asked Freddie.

DS Reid shrugged. 'Wandered round the side there.' He pointed in the direction Harrison had disappeared.

DI Painter stepped back down and looked round the side of the van. There was no sign of Harrison. He walked across to the other side and peered round. Harrison was walking slowly, eyes scanning the ground, heading towards Painter a few feet from the van.

'What are you looking for?'

'Evidence of horse hooves,' Harrison replied without looking up at him.

'And?' DI Painter asked.

There were a few moments' silence as Harrison finished his scan of the ground and eventually reached Painter and looked up.

'Nothing.'

'Right. Well, let's get inside.'

Harrison's expression caused DI Painter to pause.

'It's quite small in there, so if you don't mind, I'd like to go in alone to look around. I need to be able to concentrate and with three of us in there it's not going to work.'

'Fine. Freddie and I will go in and take a look first.'

'Please try not to move things around too much. The placement of objects can sometimes be crucial.'

DI Painter studied Harrison a moment, remembering their first encounter in the forest clearing. He'd also made a few enquiries since to get a measure of the man the NCA had sent them.

'I've heard about your reputation, Harrison. I understand that you have tracking skills and a highly perceptive eye. If you think that it will help this case if you go in first, then go ahead. Forensics have dusted and photographed, but other than that, it should be as Dax left it. Freddie and I can go in after you and have a good hunt around.'

Harrison tipped his head in thanks and appreciation.

'But if you find anything that may be material to this case, let me know immediately.'

'I will.'

* * *

Harrison stepped into the caravan and shut the door behind him. The place smelt musty and damp. He wondered how long

Dax had been living there. It would have been very cold in the winter, even with the small Calor gas stove and cooker. A duvet and sleeping bag were rumpled together on the seat that ran in a horseshoe shape around a table at the far left end of the van. To his right was a tiny kitchen, and two doors leading off at the end. Harrison stopped a moment before venturing any further. Anyone could see the furniture and decor. What he needed to see was the man who inhabited this space, and that meant studying the details.

He closed his eyes and emptied his mind, standing still for a few moments, concentrating only on his breathing. When he felt he was fully focused, he opened his eyes and look around him again.

A dirty bowl and spoon, and what looked like the dried remains of some kind of soup at the bottom, were still left out on the table. Next to this was a notepad with someone's name written down, along with a date and time. Harrison took a photograph. They'd need to check and see if this was a client or a friend. The date was for a week's time, so it was probably not the killer – but you never knew.

The note prompted Harrison to wonder how Dax ran his business. He must have a mobile phone, but how did he charge it? There was no electricity in the caravan. He made a note to raise this with DI Painter. It was possible that Wilson allowed him to charge it at his house, but if not, then where was he going to do it? And had the mobile phone been found?

Three books were also piled on the table: library copies of law textbooks, one about fighting a court case and succeeding in the criminal justice system. There'd been no mention that Dax had been in trouble with the law, but perhaps one of the protest group had been arrested. Or maybe he was arming himself with the necessary knowledge for such an encounter. If they understood the law then it was much easier to know how far they could push things before stepping over the line.

Harrison scanned the van again. Dax clearly didn't worry about housekeeping. The floor carried ample evidence of his outdoor lifestyle. A pair of wellington boots were by the door, and a set of dirty, thick gloves poked into the top of them. Harrison wondered if Dax cut back and cleared vegetation for Wilson as his way of helping out.

He moved on to the kitchen and opened the cupboards. It was clear Dax had very few possessions – and didn't keep a well-stocked kitchen. It was almost as though he didn't live full time in the caravan, but just used it as an occasional sleeping place. On the wall was a poster that had come out of a newspaper, with Britain's native trees pictured and a brief paragraph on each. The newspaper was falling victim to the damp, black mould creeping along its edges and in patches where it had touched the damp caravan wall. There were no photographs or other pictures, nothing that put Dax in a family, or told of his childhood.

Harrison approached the two doors beyond the kitchen, leading to two small bedrooms. One was empty, with just a couple of discarded carrier bags and used beer cans on the windowsill, and in the other, a double bed took up most of the space, the duvet missing and almost certainly the one scrumpled up on the seat in the main area. Peering into the shallow wardrobe, he could see a few clothes hung up, and a pair of old trainers and a bag filled with dirty laundry on the wardrobe floor. What Dax did have was mostly folded onto the stack of shelves. They were all the same: T-shirts, outdoor trousers in camouflage, or plain green or black. The bedroom window gave two small clues to Dax's character and interests: a sticker of a horned Viking helmet and another for the Woodland Trust.

The more Harrison looked around, the more he was convinced that this wasn't the only place that Dax slept. Short of tearing the place apart to find something that might be hidden, he'd seen all he could see.

As Harrison let his concentration slide, he could hear DI Painter and DS Reid talking outside. The walls of the caravan were thin.

'What do you mean, he has tracking skills?' DS Reid asked his boss in a loud whisper.

'Spent his childhood in Arizona with a Native American stepfather, apparently. He was a Shadow Wolf, one of the elite trackers who monitor the American/Mexican border. Taught him to see stuff you and I would just never see. I've heard he just walks into crime scenes and can tell you exactly what went on before forensics have even got their bags out.'

'What's a Shadow Wolf? Is that like some kind of spirit ghost?'

'No. I told you, it's a tracking unit with US Homeland Security. Look it up.'

Harrison allowed himself a small smile before returning to the fresh air outside and the expectant faces of DI Painter and DS Reid, the latter of whom had a new look of admiration on his features.

While they searched the caravan, Harrison wandered over to the cottage and knocked. Wilson Johnson answered, grumbling. He had crumbs in his beard.

'Sorry to bother you again,' Harrison said, trying to be polite and apologetic. 'But do you know if Dax stayed in the van every night?'

'I'm not his bloody dad, you know! Don't keep tabs on him – but I don't think so. He was often staying with friends and the like. You know.'

'And what about charging his phone? Did he ever ask you?'

Wilson shook his head.

'Nope.'

'Apart from Summer, did anyone else visit Dax?'

'Yeah, there was a regular group of lads, but I'm not sure about names. Summer will tell you.'

'Thank you for your time.' Harrison smiled at him.

Wilson didn't wait for him to change his mind and ask another question. He muttered something and closed the door.

Harrison walked back to the caravan just as DI Painter and DS Reid were exiting.

'Nothing.' Painter shook his head. 'Barely any personal items at all.'

Harrison agreed. 'Looks like he only used this as an occasional place to sleep.'

'So where did Mr Moore spend the rest of his time? I think we need to visit Summer and have a chat with her as soon as possible.'

9

Before they visited Summer Frances, DI Painter wanted to head back into the incident room and check on progress. Freddie was tasked with the job of phoning Summer and arranging an interview.

'Have you found Dax's mobile phone?' Harrison asked Tony.

'No. In fact, there were no personal items on his body at all. No wallet. Nothing. We only ID'd him so quickly because one constable recognised him. The killer must have taken them. The phone is turned off. Last location of it was around the woods,' DI Painter replied.

They walked back into a buzzing incident room and DI Painter headed straight to the front.

'OK, everybody, any critical updates?' The room fell silent, and the officers moved closer to Painter. 'We've just interviewed Chester Holmes. His alibi is his father, so at present, we'll keep him in the game as a potential suspect. No obvious motive, though, apart from the argument they had. He claims it was over Dax asking him if he could loan him some money for his business.'

He paused, before continuing. 'One name cropped up in

conversations with the Holmes's and also Wilson Johnson, who owns the land where Dax's caravan is parked. Summer Frances. Johnson said she read his fortune for him, and we think from his description that she might have used runes to do so. She was a good friend of Dax's, possibly more than a friend. She also has access to horses and so we're putting her top of our list and will be going to have a chat with her shortly. What do we know about Summer Frances apart from that she grooms for the Holmes family? DC Wellington, that you?' DI Painter looked at a detective who was sitting propped against one of the desks. He had a round, friendly face and a receding hairline with an oval body shape that resulted in a non-existent waistline.

'Yes,' he replied, looking to a notebook. 'She was one of those we identified as being in the victim's circle of friends. Another eco-activist. Her name came up on our database after she was arrested last year for a protest on the M4. Released with a caution. She has had quite a few different addresses over the last few years but has been in the same cottage for about eighteen months now, since she got the job grooming. No indications of serious drug issues and no other red flags from partner services.'

'Right, Sally, what have you found for us?' DI Painter asked.

The young detective constable stood up and turned to face the whole room. Harrison could see there were some nerves, but she spoke well, projecting her voice so he could clearly hear her at the back.

'I've been trying to locate every horse within a one-hour radius of the murder site. The closest, obviously, are the Holmes's horses, but there's a livery yard and riding school on the Plaistow Road side. Plus, of course, there's the Burningfold polo club and that offers liveries, which isn't too far. I've also found about four others belonging to private individuals, which are either single horses or pairs.'

'Good, then I need someone to go visit every one of these horse owners and find out if they had any connections to Dax and what they and their horses were doing at the time of his murder. The evidence definitely points to the killer being on horseback. That's a big problem for them because it helps us to narrow the field considerably. What about the spear? Who's exhibits officer?'

'That's me,' a young detective with more than a passing resemblance to Ed Sheeran raised his hand. 'Forensics say it's a home-made spear, incredibly easy to make. Someone has just cut one end of a straight branch into a point. The wood is relatively new, so anybody could have made it recently. There are no distinctive markings on the wood apart from that large arrow which had been carved into the shaft, and no fingerprints.'

'OK, disappointing, but still useful knowledge. If our killer made that spear and also took the rope to the clearing, then there is clear pre-meditated planning in this. Presume we're still waiting on DNA from the rope?'

'Yep. I put that through as an urgent so we should get something back in the next twenty-four hours.'

'I don't think it's an arrow carved into the wood,' Harrison spoke now. 'I think it's the rune, Tiwaz, which represents the battle for justice and is often thought of as the warrior rune. Norsemen would sometimes carve it into their weapons before battle.'

'More Viking mythology, but it still doesn't bring us any closer to understanding who did it,' DI Painter said, not because he was frustrated with Harrison, but with the case.

'Any luck with getting Dax's phone records?' DI Painter added.

'Still waiting, boss. The usual hoops we have to jump through to get permissions.'

'Keep up the pressure. Dax's killer had to know where he was going to be, so it's quite possible they arranged to meet at the clearing. Dr Lane, anything else of significance that we need to be chasing?'

Harrison thought for a moment.

'Odin didn't actually die by hanging and spearing himself. He found the knowledge he sought and lived on – until, that is, he was killed by a wolf. It's interesting that we keep hearing stories about a wolfman in the woods from everyone, including the man who found Dax's body. I appreciate the man has never been seen on horseback, but he's certainly an element that needs more investigation.'

'Yes, and we also can't rule out that there is more than one individual involved in this,' DI Painter prompted him.

'No, we can't. A ritual of some form had taken place prior to Dax's murder. I saw the circle that had been scraped into the earth and there was evidence of dripped candle wax. There could be a group involved. From what we saw at the scene there was no evidence of multiple individuals involved in the killing, but it can't be ruled out. I've no idea what kind of ritual it was, and so it might not even be related to Dax. The clearing is obviously a spiritual place, so it will attract those who want to be at one with nature and the trees. The wind chimes show that people visit the place, although they could be related to Dax's forest bathing business.'

'In my book, there's no such thing as coincidences,' Painter replied. 'We need to track down some former clients of his forest bathing walks. Dax was part of that eco-warrior group. I want to know everyone who was a member of it and what they've been up to. I also want to know if any other groups went to that clearing. There are druids and the like round here. Speak to all of them. What about Viking re-enactors? So far we've found no strong evidence that links Dax to Viking mythology apart from one sticker decal on his caravan window.'

'I've spoken to the dogs' team and they're going to help us tomorrow morning in the woods,' DS Reid spoke up. 'They said it's a bit of a long shot and we might need to call in some specialist search and rescue tracker dogs, but they'll do their best to see if they can find any evidence of the wolfman and where he's living. The drone is still in progress.'

'OK, everyone, keep at it. Harrison and Freddie, ten minutes' break and then we need to go see Summer Frances. Perhaps she holds the key to all this.'

10

Summer Frances lived in a terrace of tiny workman's cottages just outside the main village. Even from this distance, the forest was ever present. It could be seen like a vast land mass across the fields and Harrison would wager that on windy nights, you would be able to hear the trees bending and swaying, a vast ocean of branches and leaves.

They parked further up the street and walked along the thin pavement to the house. Summer was expecting them, and she opened the door, her eyes ringed red with emotion. DI Painter introduced each of them and she waved them in.

Summer looked to be in her mid-twenties. Her hair was shaved at the sides, and she had a long, dark-blonde plait down her back which meant she wouldn't have been out of place in a Viking movie. She was wearing a pair of tight faded jeans, with a chunky knitted cotton jumper the colour of the evergreen trees in the forest.

The house had a thin narrow entrance hall and one living room area in addition to what looked to be a small kitchen at the back of the house. The place was clean – certainly a lot cleaner than Dax's caravan had been – but it reminded Harrison of student accommodation. An eclectic mix of chairs, beanbags, and giant cushions made up the living room furniture. There was an old, small flat-screen TV. On the walls was a variety of alternative spiritual imagery: a big poster of a woman sitting in a forest and meditating; a reproduction movie poster of Chris Hemsworth as Thor; and a colourful poster of a woman wearing a long flowing dress in a wooded scene, and looking like she, too, could be a Viking warrior. Harrison recognised her to be the Norse goddess, Freyja. A small open fire was flickering, warming the room, with various chunks of wood and branches stacked on the hearth next to it.

A variety of well-read paperbacks filled the bookcase and Harrison immediately noted a ceramic statue of a horse in the middle of the top shelf. Pride of place. Next to it was a photograph of an older couple with Summer, presumably her parents.

The two detectives looked around uncertainly at the seating options: there were only three chairs; someone would have to settle with sitting on a floor cushion. DI Painter clearly decided that wasn't an option at his age, and took an armchair. Summer flopped down onto a giant red cushion, leaving the two dining table seats free for DS Reid and Harrison.

'We're sorry for your loss, Ms Frances, I understand Mr Moore was a close friend?' DI Painter started the conversation.

Tears welled in her eyes again, and she nodded.

'Yes,' she almost whispered. 'Someone said he'd been found hanging. He'd never commit suicide. You know that, right?'

'Yes. I can confirm that we're treating Dax's death as suspicious.'

Summer bowed her head and wiped her sleeve across her eyes.

'I know it's difficult to talk, but we really need as much information as possible to make it easier for us to find Dax's killer.'

She nodded, almost imperceptibly, and the DI took that as his cue to continue.

'Could you tell us a little bit more about Dax and your relationship with him?'

'Like you said, he was a good friend. We've known each other
for about five years. There's a group of us who always hang out
together.'

'Do you know if anyone had any reason to want to hurt Dax?'

Summer frowned and shook her head.

'No. He's a good bloke. He was gentle and kind. It's just crazy
that this has happened.'

'I understand that Dax sometimes went on protests. Could
he have upset anyone with his campaigning?'

'No. Our protests are peaceful. I get that they annoy people
occasionally, but he just wanted to make the world a better
place. He and Steven were always the ones in the group who
were trying to do everything legit and not resort to violence or
vandalism.'

'Steven?'

'Steven Bellowes.'

'Did this group have a name?'

'Nothing official.'

'Nothing official but—?'

'Ragnarok.'

DI Painter paused and repeated the name uncertainly,
'Ragnarok?'

'That's a pretty serious name,' Harrison joined in the conversation, guessing quite rightly that DI Painter wouldn't know the
significance of the group name. 'Ragnarok foretells the end of
the world of gods and men, doesn't it? The final battle?' He knew
what it meant, but opened up the question to hear more from
Summer.

'Yeah. It's a Norse story that tells of natural disasters and the
end of the world as we know it. That's what's coming. Global
warming is trashing the world, humans are trashing the environ-

ment, and unless we do something soon, it is going to be too late. Wildfires are getting worse, we're having weather extremes of droughts and floods, sea levels are rising, more species are going extinct, insects dying out. Soon we will have destroyed everything,' she shot back, hot passion replacing the watery tears in her eyes.

'Do what kind of something?' DI Painter picked up. 'What is it that your group does?'

'I've told you. We just protest, try to stop developments from destroying woodlands, or highlight the greed and destruction of the capitalist elite. We want to shame them, show them for what they are. There's no point just dutifully putting your recycling in the bin each week if we carry on tearing down the rainforests and polluting nature.'

'Sounds to me like that could attract the wrong kind of attention,' he pressed. 'You said Dax and Steven wanted to do everything legit, so were there others in the group who weren't? What were your most recent targets?'

'Are you here to judge our group, or are you looking for who killed Dax?' Summer clearly didn't like the focus of the questioning.

'As I said, Ms Frances, it's possible that your protests attracted the wrong kind of attention. Have any of you received threats?'

'No.'

'Who is in your group?'

Summer paused a few moments. 'Look, I don't want to get anyone into any trouble.'

'I get that, Ms Frances, but they might be able to give us some information that could help find Dax's killer. We have to pull every clue together and hope that it builds a picture of who Dax was, who he hung out with, and who might have wanted to hurt him.'

Summer shook her head and looked down at her lap.

'I don't get why anyone would want to hurt Dax. It's just crazy. Couldn't it be some random attack?'

'It might well be somebody he didn't know, but we aren't going to be able to work that out until we can piece together Dax's last movements and whether anyone had a grudge against him. When was the last time you saw him?'

'A couple of days before he died. He was fine. Not upset about anything. He was going to the library again. Dax had a crap upbringing. He was never really supported by his parents and so didn't get much of an education. He was thinking about going back to college, getting some GCSEs and stuff, and studying law.'

'Chester Holmes was seen arguing with Dax two days before he died. He said that Dax was thinking about expanding his forest bathing business, and that he'd asked him for investment. Chester thought either you or Sam Green might have suggested Dax ask him. Do you know anything about that?'

For the first time, Harrison saw an emotion other than grief on Summer's face. She didn't answer immediately. It was clear she was thinking about what Painter had just said to her.

'Yeah, now you come to mention it. He was looking to do some marketing, make a better website and stuff. So yeah, that's about right, but I didn't suggest he speak to Chester. Must have been Sam.'

Summer wrapped her arms around herself and moistened her lips. Subtle signs of a new anxiety that had taken hold of her.

'Was Dax into Viking mythology and runes?' DI Painter asked, pointing at the image of Thor on her wall.

'Do you know anything about Norse culture and mythology?' she asked, but didn't wait for his reply, assuming that DI Painter did not. 'At the centre of the universe is a tree, Yggdrasil, a sacred tree. They believed that people came from trees. They had a deep connection to them, relied on them. We just use trees now, commercialise them. We've lost our connection to the natural world because we've lived too long in our industrial landscapes. Dax understood this. He loved trees, so he found a natural affinity in the Norse culture.'

'And you?' DI Painter asked.

'My grandmother was a Norwegian Völva,' Summer said with pride and almost as a challenge to DI Painter.

'A Norse witch, or seer,' Harrison said. 'And do you have the gift?'

Summer turned to him and smiled.

'Yes. In Norway and other Nordic countries, the Viking culture and its beliefs, including witchcraft, is having a revival. In my grandmother's day, it was much harder. Now I can be open about it.' Summer sat up proudly and defiantly.

'Witchcraft?' DI Painter looked from Harrison to Summer, his face trying to contain his mild panic.

'I can see you hold the stereotypical views of a Christian.' Summer turned on Painter. 'Your religion is structured, it has only one way, and it demonises all others, calling them heathen as though it's an insult. It's not. As a Völva, I am in tune with my spiritualism, my ancestors, and with the natural world. I believe all living things are equal and no one person is better than another.'

DI Painter raised his eyebrows but kept his lips closed.

'What about the runes?' Harrison changed the subject to steer away from the conversation becoming polarised. 'Do you read them?'

'Yes, of course. I made my own set.'

Harrison looked interested.

'I'd really like to see how a rune reading works.'

It was the most animated they'd seen Summer since arriving. She got up from her red cushion and crossed to the bookcase to pick up a leather pouch.

Summer came and knelt before Harrison. As she did so, he saw a pendant around her neck.

'Is that Odin's spear on your necklace?' he asked her.

'Yes.' She smiled up at him. 'So, you need to think of something that is troubling you or for which you need some guidance. Then I cast the runes and we will see what they say to you. I'll do a quick reading, just the three. Close your eyes and concentrate on your thought.'

Harrison did as she'd asked him. He wasn't a believer in these things. He'd seen too many fortune-tellers who just fed off the information that people told them, or were excellent character judges. Yet, he couldn't help but think about the big issue in his life, the constant battle to catch his mother's killer.

'OK,' Summer began. 'We have Algiz, the elk. You stand up for things. You're a protector and that's important to you. You have strength. You also have Thurisaz, which can represent conflict, force, and fighting back, but it's angled to a reverse Othala, which is all about inheritance. Perhaps you have some legacy virtues or prejudices that are unwanted and are consuming you. I think this is a warning to not allow these to destroy you, that you must protect yourself and stand up against these inherited dangers.' Summer had been concentrating on the runes and looked up into Harrison's face. 'Does that make sense to you?'

Harrison had to remind himself to be professional and that the human mind will find purpose in random things, searching for meaning. But he had to admit that yes, what she said had made sense. DS Reid was peering at the wooden tiles she had cast, a mix of scepticism and inquisitiveness on his face.

'Did you read for Dax, or did he read them, too?' Harrison asked Summer.

'He didn't, no, but I did read for him, although not for a couple of weeks. I wish I had. Maybe there would have been a warning.'

'Can I ask you what you would make of someone receiving the three runes of Ansuz, Thurisaz, and Ehwaz?'

'As I said before, the runes can be interpreted in many ways. It depends on the individual's question and also on how they lie. Were they straight or reversed for example?'

'I understand, but the basic principles of each?'

'All I can say is that Ansuz represents Odin's wisdom, so can be about knowledge or a message. Thurisaz, as you have just received, can be a direction of force, either destruction or defence, protection or danger. And Ehwaz is the yew, the tree of life, perhaps again wisdom, or the dying of an old way and start of a new one. The life cycle.'

'Do you hold rituals at the yew tree in the woods?' Harrison asked her.

Summer's eyes narrowed and her muscles tensed.

Harrison tried to reassure her. 'I'm only asking because I saw that someone had scraped a circle with a staff and lit candles, and I notice that your thumbnail shows signs of having been burnt a little. Were you using a lighter to set fire to the candles?' Harrison gently pressed.

Summer paused, studying him. Her face showed a mix of her surprise at his observational skills, and a distrust for why he was asking her. Finally, she replied, 'Yes, it's not illegal and it's got nothing to do with Dax's death. It was a ritual blessing to keep someone safe.'

'Can I ask who?'

'It's not relevant.'

'What does this ritual consist of?' DI Painter asked.

Summer swung back round to look at him, fire in her eyes again. 'It doesn't involve sacrifices, especially human ones, if that's what you mean.'

'I wasn't inferring that, Ms Frances,' he patiently replied.

'We show our respect to nature and all living creatures,' Summer said, and then made it clear that was all she was going to say, crossing her arms and looking defiantly at the detective.

'Do you ride in the woods often? Have you ever seen anyone else around the yew tree clearing?' DI Painter changed the subject.

'Yes, I go into the woods nearly every day.'

DI Painter waited for her to continue. Harrison watched her think through what to say next and her eyes alighted on the fireplace.

'I collect wood for the fire.' She nodded towards the small open grate. 'Heating is so expensive and there's many fallen branches lying around. The main path is a good route for the horses, especially the polo ponies. Their joints often get sore with the constant turning and stopping and in the forest the path is springy.'

'Is anyone else in the group into the runes and Viking mythology?' DI Painter asked causing Summer to turn round.

'You mean, are we some kind of witch's coven?' Summer had clearly marked him as a sceptic. 'Norse witches aren't like your Halloween stories. We don't fly around on broomsticks.' Summer sighed and gave a small shiver of emotion. 'There's nobody who reads the runes like me, but Patrick's a big Viking expert. He does re-enactments and stuff.'

'Re-enactments?'

'Yeah, you know, he's in a group that gets hired by film companies and historical associations to go and stage Viking battles.'

'So, this Patrick is one of your group?' DI Painter asked.

'Yeah, but why are you all so interested in the runes and Vikings? What does this have to do with Dax's death?'

'It's just something that has come up in the course of our enquiries,' DI Painter replied.

Harrison knew that he didn't want the exact nature of Dax's death and the symbols on his chest to become public knowledge, because it was a key clue to their killer and might be useful later.

'That's just so typical. Just because you think we have different beliefs to yours, you try to blame it on that.' Summer glared at DI Painter.

'I assure you, that's not why I'm asking. Would you mind telling us about the nature of your relationship with Dax, Ms Frances?' Painter asked.

'The nature? Do you mean, were we sleeping together or just friends?'

DI Painter gave a small, patient smile.

'Everyone thought we were an item, but we weren't. We were just good mates.'

'He didn't send you that Valentine's card, then?'

Summer looked to the bookcase where a Valentine's card was displayed near to the horse statue.

'No,' was all she said and made it quite clear that this was all she would say on the subject.

'You work at the Holmes's stables as a groom?'

Summer nodded in the affirmative. 'I was there this morning.'

'What's your relationship with Chester Holmes like?'

'Why are you asking me all these questions about my relationships? Isn't this supposed to be about Dax?' Summer was becoming defensive. 'I have a lot of male friends, Sam, Patrick, Steve. They're all in our group and we hang out, I'm not sleeping with any of them. I'm not married, that's not against the law. Chester is my boss. We ride out together a lot, but he didn't know Dax or any of the others apart from Sam. So why would they get into an argument?'

'That's what we're trying to find out, Ms Frances. Perhaps it was heated enough to end in a killing?' DI Painter threw that in to see what effect it might have. His grenade exploded.

'No. Why would Chester want to hurt Dax? That's ridiculous.' Summer jumped up from her cushion and paced the room.

'How about the wolfman in the forest? Have you seen him?'

Her arms wrapped around her body again, and she turned away from DI Painter.

'That's just gossip. Look, if you don't mind, I'm kind of wiped out. Is that it now?'

'We are asking everyone who knew Dax to tell us where they were that evening and late afternoon.'

'You mean, do I have an alibi?' She swung back round, defensive again. 'You don't seriously think I'd hurt him? He was my friend. Just because I don't prescribe to your authoritarian set of beliefs and lifestyle doesn't mean to say I'm a killer.'

'I'm sorry if you think that I was in any way suggesting that, Ms Frances. I assure you that I am not making any judgement on your beliefs or lifestyle. We are asking everyone who knows Dax. It helps us to build up a picture of who was where when he was murdered.' Harrison heard the practised patience and calming tone of a seasoned detective in DI Painter's reply.

'I was here. On my own. I'd been at the stables all day and came home exhausted, had a hot bath and chilled.'

'No problem, that's helpful to know.'

DI Painter stood up, and DS Reid and Harrison followed suit.

'I'm sorry we've taken up so much of your time in these difficult circumstances, but just one last quick question. Did Dax leave any belongings here? We didn't find much at the caravan.'

She shook her head, then added, 'He wasn't really a possessions kind of guy. He occasionally did his washing here, that's about it.'

'Is there anything here now?'

'No.'

'OK, thank you. And would you mind giving us the contact

details for the other three friends you mentioned?' DI Painter consulted his notebook. 'Sam, Patrick, and Steven.'

'I guess. They're on my phone.'

While Summer was busy giving the three numbers to the DI, Harrison crossed over to the bookshelf and looked at the Valentine's card. *To my Frigg, from your Thor.*

Whoever had sent it could be as passionate about Vikings as Summer, or they might simply be playing to her interests. One thing that was clear to Harrison was that Summer was holding back on something, but he wasn't yet sure what.

11

DS Reid worked fast and had Sam Green's address within five minutes of leaving Summer's house. He'd definitely calmed down since Harrison had first met him in the clearing. There were no more insensitive jibes and he was working hard.

'He's got some previous,' Reid said to his boss.

'Find out if he's at work. If not, let's go round there now and pay him a surprise visit.'

Harrison checked his own phone while he waited. He'd received a text when he was in Summer's house and didn't recognise the number.

Enjoying Surrey and West Sussex? was all it said.

Harrison thought about who it could be for a few moments, but then decided to wait and see if they sent another message that might reveal their identity. As they drove to Sam's, he was concentrating on DI Painter and DS Reid's conversation in the front of the car and thinking through everything that Summer had just told them.

He'd just slipped his phone back into his pocket when it buzzed again.

It was a photograph this time. A shot of Tanya. Only this

wasn't a selfie that she'd sent to him with love. This was a picture taken from a distance by somebody she clearly didn't know was there. She was walking along the street towards her flat in London, and she was carrying the small bag she'd taken on their weekend away.

Harrison's heart seemed to stop beating for a few moments and then started again at four times the speed. Who was this? Was this a joke?

A second photograph arrived. This time it was of both of them sitting by a window in the hotel yesterday morning. Again, the shot had been taken by a telephoto lens from a distance. There was a roaring in Harrison's ears. He felt sick. He stared at the photograph, feeling violated and vulnerable.

Then, a fourth text. *Stick to the day job, Dr Lane. We're watching.*

It was a clear threat, echoing the last words that DCI Lynne Turner had said to him before she was taken away and charged with perverting the course of justice. While he'd been helping investigate some murders and the burning of churches just before Christmas, she'd been the lead detective on the case and had threatened him, telling him, 'You're being watched.'

Whoever it was that had killed his mother didn't want him investigating her death and the DCI had been part of their evil network. Harrison hadn't any idea of just how far that network spread within the police, but it couldn't be coincidental that these photographs were taken the day after he'd spoken to Inspector Rob Morgan. No doubt he'd received similar threats which suggested Harrison's mother's killer was even more powerful than he'd anticipated.

Anger coursed through every molecule in his body. He felt like a kettle bubbling and boiling inside. Every muscle taut. Elastic bands stretched and ready to snap. He wasn't afraid of them, but he'd created a weakness, a vulnerability they could exploit. All these years he'd avoided relationships for fear of something like this. Tanya was now in danger because of him. Only last year she'd been attacked by a stalker who had latched onto her after meeting her at a crime scene. She'd endured weeks of fear knowing that she was being watched. Now, she was under surveillance again, her privacy violated, and it was his fault.

His mother's killer was forcing him to make a choice between justice for his mother, or the woman he loved.

12

___

Summer Frances had watched through the window as the three police officers walked up the road and drove off. She was a whirlpool of grief. She took out her phone and flicked through some of her photographs. Dax's kind eyes smiled back at her, and she could almost hear his laughter. The warmth of his personality and his passion for his beloved trees. Why would anyone want to hurt him?

The police detective was just like so many people, set in his views, blind to what was around him. The blinkers he wore meant she didn't have much faith in him finding out who had murdered Dax and why. She would consult the runes later, but right now, she didn't have the answer to her questions. What she did know was that it had something to do with what Dax had been working on at the library.

He'd been excited about something when she'd last seen him. More positive than he'd been in a long time. He told her that he might have a solution to the dilemma which had vexed him for the past eighteen months. Kind and passionate Dax. He'd shared his secret with her a few months ago. Could that somehow have led to his death?

She and Dax had been careful to never mention the secret via text or any kind of traceable message, or to write anything down, but could Dax's research have led him to a discovery that someone didn't want revealed?

There was only one way for her to find out, and that was to go to the library and look at what he'd been researching. She'd no doubt that the murderer would have taken his bag with his phone and notebook and all his notes, otherwise the police would have mentioned something.

Summer grabbed her shoes, coat, and bag and hurried out of her little cottage. Her car was parked just down the road. She could get to the library with a couple of hours to spare before closing, if she hurried. Dax was gone, but there was another life at risk and now it was up to her alone to ensure they were protected.

13

'Harrison? Dr Lane, are you coming?'

Harrison was staring out the window of the car, not focusing on where he was, but on the turmoil in his mind.

'Harrison, we've arrived at Sam Green's. Is everything alright?'

DI Painter's voice cut through into Harrison's consciousness, and he snapped back into the moment. They were pulled over in a residential parking area below a block of flats. He looked at Painter's concerned face.

'Are you alright, Dr Lane?' the detective asked again.

'Sorry, I'm fine,' he replied and opened the car door to join them, trying to shake off the feelings of violation and anger which were coursing through him. What he really wanted to do was to walk in the opposite direction. Go and find his Harley and ride straight home to London, where he could protect Tanya. Would they really hurt her? Was she in danger now? He'd weighed through the issue in his mind as they'd driven and decided that she was safe. They wouldn't hurt her unless he went up against them again because she was their only bargaining chip. That had made him feel better. The fact it meant he wouldn't be able to still investigate his mother's murder was a problem he'd have to think about at another time. Harrison gave himself a mental shake and tuned into the two detectives he was with.

'So, Sam Green didn't go into work yesterday or today. Phoned in sick, apparently,' DS Reid was telling them. 'That's why we need to speak to him now. It could just be that he was shocked about Dax's death – that wouldn't be unheard of as they were mates – but his name has been mentioned by Chester and Summer, so I figured it's important for us to explore his whereabouts further.'

'Not a bad little block of flats for a delivery driver,' DI Painter noted.

Harrison realised he'd not looked at his surroundings at all. He gave himself another mental slap and forced himself to concentrate on the here and now. To put his own personal issue to one side. This was what they would enjoy, seeing him struggle to do his job properly. For them to know that they'd got to him. He wasn't going to give them that satisfaction and he didn't want to let anyone down, least of all Dax Moore.

The flats were a relatively new build. Red brick with small balconies for each apartment. Only four levels high, not a big tower block, and it was a tasteful entrance that looked well maintained. The cars in the car park were those which would easily pass an MOT and the furniture and decorations on the various balconies showed that these were properties people cared about. It was also the first place Harrison had been to where he couldn't see the forest. The trees were lost behind buildings that rose up all around them, their song drowned by the noise of traffic.

The front door was locked, and a keypad their mode of entry, so DS Reid rang Sam's flat to request access.

'Yeah?' a young man's voice came through the speakerphone.

'Mr Samuel Green? It's the police. We're hoping to have a word with you, please?'

There was no answer.

'Mr Green?'

'Yeah, why?'

'We just wanted to ask you a few questions about Dax Moore. We understand you're a friend of his?'

'Yeah. That's right.' There was a pause. 'OK.'

The buzzer to give them access to the building sounded, and DS Reid pushed the door open. Just as they were walking in, Harrison saw the balcony doors in one of the first-floor flats opened wide, although he didn't see anyone come out.

'You take the lead on this one,' DI Painter said to DS Reid as they walked up one flight of stairs. 'He sounds like he might relate more to your age group than mine.'

Harrison followed behind, a sick feeling in his gut that made his stomach feel like he'd swallowed a ball of rusty iron wool.

'You sure you're alright, Harrison?' DI Painter asked as they reached number six and DS Reid knocked.

'Fine,' he replied, but gave no further explanation. That was not a conversation for this occasion. He gave himself an internal pep talk, forcing his mind to focus despite the dull spinning pain that had settled in his head.

DI Tony Painter gave him a look that said he wasn't convinced, but let it drop.

The three of them waited for the door to be opened, but Sam didn't immediately appear. Freddie turned round and raised his eyebrows.

'Reckon he's doing a bit of a tidy up in there.'

The faint sounds of activity filtered through the door.

They waited a few more moments, before DS Reid added, 'Wonder what he's tidying away!' and knocked again.

A few moments later, a lock was turned, and the door flung open. Sam was a young man in his early thirties, wearing jogger pants and a Nike hoodie. He sported short, cropped hair around the back and side of his head, with a longer nest of dark blond on top that looked like it hadn't been brushed that day. He was unshaven, Harrison estimated around two days' worth of stubble, although because he was blond and fine-haired, it had the effect of making him look more like a trendy version of Shaggy from *Scooby Doo* than an action hero. By far the most remarkable thing about his appearance was the split lip and bruising to his face, including a black eye. The injuries looked a couple of days old.

'Wasn't expecting visitors,' Sam said to them as he led them into his flat.

The reason for his panicked tidying became apparent, when despite the open balcony doors, the distinct whiff of marijuana met them.

Sam crossed to the doors and shut the cold out.

DS Reid introduced them all and they sat down in the living room area that fed off the kitchen diner. It was a distinct change to Summer's house, a sparsely decorated bachelor pad with a signature black wall and cream paint throughout. No pictures or photographs on the walls. A large wide-screen TV, which must have been around fifty-five inches, dominated the room, and white leather sofas were horseshoe-shaped around it. Sam sat down and they followed his lead.

'I heard about Dax,' Sam started. 'A right shock.' He looked genuinely upset as he said it.

'We understand you were good friends with Dax?' Freddie started.

'Yeah. We hung out most weeks. He was an alright dude.'

Sam's right leg started to jiggle up and down.

'When did you last see Dax?'

Sam licked his lips and turned to stare out the window.

'Um, think it was just before the weekend... Yeah, Wednesday or Thursday.' Sam turned back to look at Freddie.

Harrison didn't miss the slight shoulder shrug and his hands rubbing his thighs for comfort. He was nervous, and he was lying. Sam had tried to cover his right hand up to this point, but clearly his nerves made him forget, and Harrison saw the grazes and bruises on his right knuckles.

'How was he? Was he worried about anything or being threatened by anyone?' Freddie continued.

'No. No, not that he told me. He was fine.'

His answer was more positive, but Harrison wondered if he was talking about another occasion that they'd met up, rather than the most recent one.

'Do you know if Dax was seeing anyone? We've been round to his caravan, and it doesn't look like he sleeps there much.'

'I think he spends a lot of time at Summer's place,' Sam replied. 'They're not, like, officially girlfriend, boyfriend, but I think they do get together. If you know what I mean?'

'I see,' Freddie replied. 'She's into all her Viking stuff, isn't she? Read the runes, I think they're called, while we were there. She ever done that for you?'

'Yeah, I don't, like, take loads of notice of 'em. But it keeps her happy, like. Don't believe in any of that. Her, Dax, and Patrick are into all the Viking stuff, but I ain't that bothered about history. What's gone is gone. They reckon trees should be sacred. I just think we need 'em to breathe.'

'I understand you're part of the Ragnarok group with Dax and Summer?'

'Yeah, I join 'em for protests and stuff, but I'm not as into it all as they are.'

'Sorry, in what way are they more into it than you, Sam?'

'Like I told ya: Dax with his forest bathing, Summer with her spiritual stuff. I just think it's shite the way big business gets to trash the environment and we all have to suffer.'

'Is it possible that something the group has done could have angered somebody enough to get Dax killed?'

'Dunno, maybe. Patrick's a bit more radical. He was always trying to push us to do more stuff.'

'Did Dax want to push the boundaries, too?'

'Not really. He and Steve were always talking Patrick down. Summer just went along with the flow. None of them ever said nothing to me about any particular grief.'

'You said Summer is more spiritual. Did you participate in any of her rituals?'

'Rituals? Makes it sound like some kind of Satanic thing. She used to do some blessing things before we went out on a protest, said she was getting the spirits to protect us and bring us success. Can't say that I took much notice or that they ever made much difference.'

'Were these in the forest?'

Reid looked at Harrison as though trying to gauge if he wanted to step in with any questions. 'I think she might have with Dax, they were always in the forest, but I only saw them when I was at Dax's caravan, or hers.'

'Do you mind me asking how you got the injuries?' Reid nodded towards Sam's black eye and cut lip.

He shrugged. 'Just a bit of a bust up in the pub. You know how it is.'

'Oh, which pub was that?'

'Which pub? Well, it weren't actually in the pub, it was after I'd left.'

'Was Dax with you?'

'No.'

'When was this?'

'Err, couple of days ago, I think.'

'A couple of days? The day that Dax was murdered?'

'No. Friday. It was the day before.'

'But you didn't see Dax that day?'

Sam shook his head and gave another small shrug of his shoulders.

'Which pub was it?' Freddie tried again.

'Dog and Ball, but like I said, it was after I'd left that they jumped me.'

'And you didn't report it?'

'Nah. It happens, right? I didn't know who they were. Never seen 'em before. I was alright.'

'Do you know what they wanted? Did they steal anything?'

'No. Nothing. They were just tanked and did it for kicks, I guess. Might have thought I had cash on me cos I do deliveries. Yeah, that was probably it.'

Freddie let it drop, but Harrison could see that he was of the same opinion as he was. He didn't believe Sam's account of that night at all.

'We're asking everyone who knew Dax to tell us where they were at the time of his murder. It helps us to place everyone. Can you tell us where you were between the hours of five p.m. and ten p.m. on Saturday?'

'I was delivering until about nine, then came home. I was going to go to the pub, but I was too knackered.'

'Delivering cupcakes?'

'Yeah. People want them for parties and stuff, and are out during the weekdays, so they want them delivered in the evenings or at weekends. It's next day delivery on orders and we've been right busy.'

'So, you work for Chester Holmes, don't you?' He changed tack.

'Yeah.'

'Do you know what kind of relationship he had with Dax?'

'Relationship?' Sam looked a little confused.

'Yeah, I mean, were they friends? Did they know each other?'

'Oh, right. No, not really. I never saw 'em together.'

'There's been a suggestion that Dax was looking to expand his forest bathing business and possibly you suggested that he ask Chester about investing in it?'

Sam frowned and shook his head.

'Don't know nothing about that. Not really Chester's bag, so I wouldn't have said anything.'

'Were you aware that Chester and Dax had an argument on the Friday before he died?'

Sam shook his head and shrugged again.

'Chester or Dax never mentioned it?'

'Not to me. No.' Sam looked from one man to the next as though butter wouldn't melt in his mouth.

'Do you ride horses, Mr Green? Ever ridden one of the boss's?'

'I started as a groom for Chester. Didn't you know that? That's how Summer and I first met. So yeah, I've ridden his horses, but not lately. Prefer sticking to the mopeds now, less temperamental, and they don't need mucking out.'

'I can see why that's a more attractive job,' DS Reid smiled at him. 'So, you've definitely no idea who or why anyone would want to hurt your friend?'

'No.'

'OK. Thank you for your time. If you think of anything that might help us with the investigation, please do get in touch.'

'And if you want us to pursue charges against the men who attacked you, we can look into that, too,' DI Painter added, staring Sam in the face.

'Yeah. OK. Cheers.'

All four of them stood up and started to move towards the front door.

'Nice place you've got,' Painter said to him casually, smiling.

'Yeah, cheers. Bought it last year.'

Sam's face had noticeably relaxed at the prospect of the three of them leaving. Harrison looked around the flat as much as he could on their way to the exit, trying to get a measure of Sam Green. He saw nothing that could link to their case, just a regular modern bachelor's pad – apart from the row of cannabis bongs, in different shapes and colours, that ran along the kitchen windowsill where most people would have plant pots.

As soon as they were back in the car and well out of earshot, DI Painter turned to them both and raised his eyebrows.

'Well, a big chunk of that was a pack of lies. What do we make of Sam Green?'

'Don't believe a word of the fight story,' DS Reid offered, starting the engine.

'No. So was the fight connected to Dax? Could whoever beat Sam up have then gone on to kill Dax?'

'Maybe, but if so, why's Sam lying? Why not tell us and catch his friend's killers?'

'Maybe he's been threatened. He's scared and doesn't want to be next. Could also explain why he's holing up in his flat. We need to get on to the cupcake company and find out what his shift was on the day Dax was killed and also go to the pub and find out if he really did go in there for a pint. Look for CCTV around the pub, too, and on his route home. Those are all main roads so there's a strong chance this so-called attack might have been captured.'

'Definite smell of ganja in that flat, too. Do you reckon he's dealing? Can't see how a cupcake delivery driver affords a place like that,' Reid added.

'My thoughts exactly. We need to do full background checks on Mr Green. And make a few more enquiries about Dax's lifestyle. If Sam is dealing and he's friends with Dax, it's not a big leap to consider his death could be drug gang related.'

'Unlikely. It's much more personal than that.' Harrison spoke for the first time since they'd arrived.

DI Painter turned round in his seat to look at Harrison, and DS Reid's gaze moved to the rear-view mirror.

'I agree that it's not your usual drug turf killing. They're usually quick and straightforward, execution style, but we can't rule it out,' DI Painter replied. 'Could be trying to make a statement.'

'He's not been killed in a turf war. This is something much more personal to the killer. He's taken a great deal of care to stage Dax's death, and plan it. Those runes carved on his chest were chosen with some thought. The spear and the tree all have meaning.'

'Maybe. Or we could be wasting our time looking for a motive and it's just some psycho wolfman in the woods who took a dislike to Dax,' Reid offered.

'Well, it's getting late now, and we need to follow up the leads we have. Let's get back to the office and start gathering some more information. Harrison, what do you want to do?' Painter asked him.

'I need to write up a full profile and report for you and then, after that we can assess if I'm still needed. I'll stay locally for tonight.'

'OK. We'll have a briefing first thing, eight thirty. It would be good to have you there for that.'

Harrison nodded his agreement. He'd write up what he'd come here for and then see if he could leave them to it. He was being mentally and emotionally tortured by the text messages, just as they'd intended. He needed to get back to London and deal with the situation before it drove him crazy.

14

Sam Green let out a huge breath of relief after he'd closed the door on the police detectives. He'd been worried they might ask to search the flat if they smelt the ganja. Had they believed him about his injuries?

Sam went into the bathroom and put the toilet lid down before climbing onto it. Then he reached up above his head and nudged the ceiling tile up before sliding it aside. His fingers felt for the small phone, reminding him as he searched that his knuckles were bruised and sore.

He found it and sat down on the toilet lid to make the call. They'd need to know that the police were sniffing around.

It was time to do a little bit of spring cleaning.

15

Harrison booked into a local budget hotel. It would be a big step down from the opulent traditional luxury of where he'd stayed the previous night, but the standardised anonymity would be welcome.

He'd managed to pay attention long enough in the interview with Sam Green to be able to make some observations, but Harrison knew that his concentration was shot. His brain was overloaded and on go-slow. He needed to clear his mind and stop his personal problems from impacting on his work.

Harrison's usual cure for anger and frustration was to run himself so hard that he drained the pent-up energy and flooded his body with endorphins. This time, that wasn't going to be a solution. The turmoil in his brain had leached into his muscles, which felt lethargic. There was also a feeling he had which he hadn't experienced in a long time. One which it had taken him all afternoon to fathom. He felt scared. Not for himself, but for those closest to him.

The conversation with Rob Morgan made total sense now. Rob would have received a similar threat, and he'd quite naturally chosen to protect his family. Harrison certainly couldn't blame him.

For the first time since he was a teenager, Harrison was tempted to get to his hotel and go straight to the bar and order a double whisky or two. It would be an easy relief. Take the edge off the feelings consuming his mind and body, to allow him some release. He was tempted, but there was no way he was going to follow through. He wouldn't compromise himself for them.

Instead, he did what he always did when he found his mental and emotional self drained: he turned to nature. Before he checked into his hotel, Harrison returned to the car park at the woods that he'd gone to yesterday. He was going to walk to the yew tree again, ground himself in nature, and now that it was quiet and there were no emergency services personnel there, he'd be able to get a real feel for the place before he wrote his report.

To begin with, his mind still whirred with his own thoughts. He walked but he wasn't connecting with his surroundings; he was focused on internal struggles. The words of his old friend Professor Andrew McKendrick had come back to him. He'd warned him not to stir up a hornet's nest. Told him to put the past behind him and focus on those who were threatening people today.

Harrison hadn't visited Andrew since he'd discovered that he'd known his mother when they were both younger, and never told him. All the years that he was his mentor at university and long after, he never once mentioned that they'd been friends and that she'd asked him to keep an eye out for Harrison. He'd only found out accidentally. The bond of trust had been broken, and Harrison had found it hard to forgive him.

Harrison missed him, though. Missed their deep philosophical conversations about religion in the older man's home office. He'd felt safe there, surrounded by books and familiarity. A home from home. Perhaps Andrew could still help him. Maybe he didn't know the full picture, but perhaps he could remember some of the people who were in his mother's life at the time. Then Harrison could follow the trail.

What was he thinking? There he was again, like a rabid dog on the scent of something. If he continued to keep digging, then he would be putting Tanya's life in danger. He had no idea who in the police were connected to the network that his mother's killer controlled. For that reason it was also out of the question to ask his friend, Detective Sergeant Jack Salter, to help him, because they'd no doubt be alerted when he started asking the wrong questions. Jack was going to have to stay well out of it. He had his family to consider.

Harrison had options for investigation, but every way he turned, he knew that they would trace it back to him, and that was a direct threat to Tanya. He could end his and Tanya's relationship, but that wouldn't be enough. They'd anticipate that move and they wouldn't be fooled. Even if he said he'd never see her again, if they caught him investigating, then they would make her the target because they knew that would hurt him the most, unless he ended it now and then waited a year or two before continuing the investigation. Put some time and distance between them which would keep her safe. It would give her the chance to meet a more regular guy who could be there for her every day. He could never give up his job and that meant travelling around the country and spending long periods away from home. He wasn't being fair on her. Being with him put her in danger. She deserved better. It was the right thing to do.

Harrison was about halfway to the clearing when he stopped, the weight of the dilemma pressing down on him. He could feel his heart pounding in his chest and the pressure in his head threatening to bring on another headache. He'd come here to clear his mind and regain his focus, reconnect with the world.

He was doing anything but that. This was a problem that couldn't be solved in one day. His best option was to do nothing for now, keep Tanya safe until he'd returned to London and had time to think.

Coming to that conclusion helped. While it might just be putting off a bigger decision, it at least reduced the pressure. He felt the floodgates of emotion open and looked around himself properly for the first time. There was no one in sight. That didn't surprise him as walkers had probably been put off coming into the woods following the murder. It wouldn't be long before dusk and an active imagination in a dark forest was a potent combination.

He closed his eyes and focused on his breathing, connecting with all his senses. Deep breaths in. The smell and taste of the pine trees and rotting leaves of the deciduous trees. Deep breaths out. The sound of a bird's wings flapping as it took off from a tree close by.

The high-pitched chirrup of starlings. A musical verse from a red-breasted robin, the beautiful lyrical sound probably hiding a more sinister motive, acting as a warning to any other robins that this territory was his.

Slowly, Harrison felt his body relax. His shoulders drop, his heart rate slow. He opened his eyes and looked at the huge brown and green trees rising up above his head all around him. He looked down and imagined the huge mycorrhizal fungi networks beneath his feet, connecting the trees so they can share food and communicate with each other – the wood wide web. He saw a big domed pile of twigs, leaves and pine needles to one side of the path, an area less shaded by trees. It was a southern wood ant nest, its occupants just getting ready to start their spring cycle of life. Tens of thousands of ants all working together as one big community to serve their queens.

All around him there was life, some silent and invisible,

some obvious and vocal. Some warm blooded and breathing in oxygen, some harnessing the sun and creating it. All existing together, creating the diversity of life on earth. Harrison was just one more living organism. This was what Summer meant, the Norsemen's belief systems. They understood and connected with their world. They weren't just about invading and pillaging; nature was essential to them. They lived in it, off it, sometimes worshipped it. They knew that humans were in many ways the dominant living creatures, but that nature was more powerful. That upsetting the balance could risk everything. This was how Summer felt and this innate love of the forest was also Dax's. So, who would find that threatening enough to kill him?

Harrison started walking again, but this time he looked around him and he listened.

Suddenly, just ahead to his right, he heard the screeching warning calls of birds along with flapping in the treetops as the alarm sent them flying off. He stopped, eyes scanning the trees for movement. The forest faded into grey as the weak daylight dimmed. He thought he saw the flash of something running across. It was a dark shape, too far away for him to see clearly. He thought about running after them, getting a better look. It could be the wolfman, or it could be their murderer come back to the crime scene. But Harrison knew they were too far ahead for him to catch up and tracking them in the fading light would be slow and difficult. They'd be long gone.

Instead, he carried on walking, only now there was an edge in the air. A feeling that the natural order had been disturbed. A vapour trail left across the surface of the wood.

As Harrison walked into the clearing and was faced by the yew tree, an unexpected sight met his eyes. Attached to the trunk of the ancient tree were photographs.

He walked forward, being careful to scan the ground in case he walked through any potential evidence. As he got closer, he could see they were all images of the same person. The smiling face of Dax Moore looked out at him, reminding Harrison that a young man was lying in the morgue, his life cut short and somewhere, someone clearly missed him.

16

The dark shadow in the forest had seen the big man before he saw him. He recognised him as being with the police. He saw a lot of what went on around the woods. His woods.

He'd not stayed, fearful that if he saw him then he might get caught. Be sent back. The trees were his home, his guardians. Deep in the woods he could avoid them. Hide.

Violence had once been his every day. A constant companion to fear in his old life. In the woods he had found sanctuary. The trees spoke to him, singing of the power of nature, protecting and nurturing. He had found his peace. Until now. The violence had returned and invaded the sacred heart of his home. It twisted around his insides and gnawed at his spirit with its rabid hunger.

He had to fight back.

17

Summer had just got back from the library when the police called her. It was Detective Sergeant Freddie Reid.

'Ms Frances, apologies to disturb you again, but have you been to the yew clearing and left photographs of Dax on the tree? Just to be clear if you have, you're not in any trouble, we're just trying to ascertain who might have done so as we piece together who was in Dax's life.'

'No. No it wasn't me,' Summer replied.

The detective had thanked her and rung off.

Summer knew who had left the photographs, but she wasn't about to tell the police that information. She imagined they would call all of their Ragnarok group, but it would lead them nowhere. Besides, Summer had more important things to think about. At the library, she'd scanned the book that the librarian told her Dax had asked for three days ago. At first she thought it had been a wasted journey. A dead end. Then it had jumped out at her from the pencil drawn map, roughly sketched of the woods. Was this the knowledge that had led to Dax's death? With just two sentences in the text referring to it, how could something that seemed so small lead to such big consequences? Why was it so important?

As she sat there thinking through its meaning, a far darker thought came into her mind. If this was the reason, then it could only lead to one person. Only one individual who could possibly want this kept hidden from the world.

Summer had put the book back on the shelf and slipped out of the library into the fast-approaching night. Her legs felt slightly weak at the discovery. She had toyed with the idea of telling the Detective Sergeant what she'd found. Ask them to investigate. But her heart fought with her mind. Before going to the authorities, she had to ask him about it. There was probably a rational explanation, and he would be able to tell her that he hadn't known about it either. That it was nothing to do with him or Dax's death.

Summer pulled her mobile phone from her pocket and dialled his home number.

18

The next day, Harrison woke up with a headache, which wasn't a great way to start a fasting day, but he took some paracetamol with water and checked out of the hotel. He intended to go to the morning briefing, give his report, and then head back to London in the afternoon. Ryan had done a sterling job of holding the fort while he'd been away at the weekend, but there were a couple of other cases that needed his professional input and it looked like he'd done as much as he could with this one.

The incident room was buzzing when he got there and it was standing room only, which suited him just fine. Harrison took up his usual position at the back of the room, leaning against the wall. A female police officer in her early thirties came and stood next to him. She tried to catch his eye a few times and smiled. Harrison stayed focused on the front of the room, oblivious.

DI Painter put his cup of coffee down and clapped his hands for quiet.

'Let's get started,' he said to the room. 'We've made some progress, but we're no closer to finding Dax's killer, and there are still several lines of inquiry which we need to concentrate on today. We still don't have a solid motive. I want no stone unturned in looking at Dax Moore's life and acquaintances. We know he had no criminal record, apart from a caution at a protest. So, who could have wanted to kill a man who we keep being told was a lovely guy who was passionate about trees and nature; who was a vegan pacifist who disliked violence and yet he had an argument the day before he was killed?'

The room murmured at the last comment as all the bacon and beefburger lovers voiced their usual opinion on veganism.

Painter continued. 'Was it somebody who took offence at their protests? This group, Ragnarok, I want somebody checking to see if there's anything we can find about what they've been up to. How radical were they? We've spoken to Summer and Sam who are in the group, but if they're breaking the law, then they're not going to volunteer that information to us. Then there's the Viking elements of the murder. Dr Lane, do you have anything else you'd like to add for us, especially after visiting Summer Frances yesterday? I'm particularly interested in the witchcraft side of things.'

Another murmur went round the room at the mention of witchcraft.

'Yes. I think it's important to be clear about what we're not talking about as well as what we are dealing with. Summer is not a witch in the Christian sense of the meaning. Viking Völvas came before our more traditional view of a witch. Völva actually means wand or magic staff carrier. They practised a magic called Seidr and were prophets and healers who were important in their communities. They were said to be able to influence battles. Sam mentioned that Summer used to do some kind of ritual before they went on their protests, a kind of modern day battle, if you like, over the environment. There was also evidence of a ritual having taken place in the yew clearing where Dax was murdered.'

'I thought Vikings sacrificed people? I've seen that on TV in *The Last Kingdom*,' a uniformed officer said.

'There were human sacrifices, yes, but Dax's murder didn't look to me like a sacrifice. Sacrifices to the spirits would generally involve bloodletting, or fire. We can't rule it out but, in the clearing, we didn't find evidence of a group of people being involved in his killing. It was more like a punishment or revenge. I think we also need to find out who sent Summer that Valentine's card. It said to Frigg, from Thor. Frigg was the goddess of love and sexuality, as well as prophecy. She was also wife to Odin. Thor was god of thunder, sacred groves, strength, and protector of humans. We need to find out who thinks he is Thor and whether he has decided to protect Summer from something or someone, or has an over-inflated view of himself. We need to also keep in mind that although Summer has denied having a sexual relationship with Dax, Sam seemed to think they were an item.'

'So you're saying you think this could be a love triangle?' Painter asked.

'It's possible. I'm not saying it is, but I think we need to keep our minds open and not just assume it has something to do with the protest group. It might involve people from the group, but not because of their campaigns. As you know, crime is so often prompted by simple human emotions.'

'And don't forget Chester Holmes, who has the Bemford Cupcake business,' Painter added. 'According to both Summer and Sam, the pair didn't really know each other, had nothing in common, and yet we know that they were seen arguing the day before Dax was killed. Chester said it was because Dax had asked him to invest in his forest bathing business. He'd declined. Is he telling the truth? Chester's alibi is his father, so it's not rock solid, and Chester also happens to have four horses, which he rides regularly.'

DI Painter flipped the image on the screen in front of them, and Summer's face appeared.

'Summer Frances, our Viking Völva, works for Chester as a

groom. She's also a great friend of Dax's. As Harrison said, we're not entirely sure how great, but he spends a lot of time away from his caravan, so is he staying with her? Summer uses runes, which are the symbols found carved into Dax, to tell peoples' prophecies, so she's a link to the symbols and imagery used in Dax's murder. Like Chester, she rides horses, and she also doesn't have a solid alibi for the time of Dax's murder.'

The screen changed again to show a scowling Sam Green from a police arrest photo.

'Sam Green is a friend and member of Dax and Summer's Ragnarok group. He also works for Chester as a delivery driver. He's got minor convictions for shoplifting and for breach of the peace. But nothing in the last few years. He was in a fight the day before Dax's murder. We need to find out with who and why. We're checking out his alibi. He also lives in a property which should be out of the range of a delivery driver's salary. How did he afford it? There was a distinct smell of ganja in his flat when we visited, so is Sam Green somehow involved in drugs? Did Dax find out about this and that's why he's dead? Sam was a former groom of Chester Holmes and so is perfectly capable of riding a horse.'

'Next up we have Patrick Sheldon, ex-army, a couple of minor convictions, including one for assault. He's also a Viking re-enactor, really into them apparently, and likes dressing up and recreating battles. Part of the Ragnarok group and apparently keen to get more serious with their environmental fight-back. So, did something go wrong with their relationship? He has to be priority number one today, not least because of his military background and Viking interests.'

The screen changed again to show a photo that looked like it had been taken from a driver's licence.

'Steven Bellowes, clean as a whistle, but he hangs out with the rest of them and tries to save the world. Is he hiding a dark side? We need to pay him a visit. Plus, we also have a wild card in the mix.'

Tony flipped the image one final time to show a photofit of a man with shoulder length, dark hair and a beard.

'This is wolfman. There have been countless sightings of this man, who some people say is half wolf and half man, in the woods. He's even said to have killed a sheep with his bare hands and savagely ripped it to pieces. We can discount the wildest rumours, but what if someone is living rough in the forest? The man who discovered Dax's body saw someone of this description running away from the scene. Now Dax was long dead by this point, but did he have anything to do with it? Do we have someone with a mental illness living in the woods?

'Dax spent a lot of time in the forest, so maybe somehow this man felt threatened, or he just decided to kill. We need to know more about this mystery man. We've got a dog team on its way to the forest right now, and I want all sightings of wolfman gathered together so we can separate the facts from the local mythology.'

DI Painter's mobile phone started to ring. He took it out of his pocket without looking at it and silenced it, placing it on a desk where it continued to vibrate.

'I'm going to go and visit Patrick Sheldon this morning, but I want more effort on finding out every background detail of the names on this board, who they hang out with—'

DI Painter hesitated as DS Reid's mobile started to ring. Freddie gave him an apologetic look and slipped off to the side of the room to take the call.

DI Painter continued. 'Yesterday, late afternoon, Dr Lane went back to the crime scene in the forest and found that somebody had pinned photographs to the yew tree Dax was found hung on. Like some kind of tribute or shrine. Summer has denied doing this, so I want to know who put them there. See if you can track down where they might have been printed off. Get the paper analysed—'

'Sir. Sir.' DS Freddie Reid had a hand raised and the mobile phone still at his ear.

DI Painter and the rest of the room hushed and looked at him. It was obvious from his body language and the expression on his face that somebody was telling him something important.

'OK. We're leaving now,' Freddie said to the caller. 'It's the dog team,' he said to DI Painter. 'They've found another body.'

19

DI Painter, Harrison, DS Reid, and DC Gorman blue-lighted their way to the forest.

'No details yet, but there are symbols cut into them like with Dax,' DS Reid told them in the car. 'Forensics have just arrived,' he added as DI Painter flung them all towards the passenger side of the car as he overtook a learner driver and wove between the traffic.

'Same location?' Harrison asked.

'No. Apparently not far from the car park area. People have been avoiding the woods since the murder, and with the stories of the wolfman circulating, it's scared the public away. The dog team had only been there five minutes when one of the dogs found the body.'

The car park was buzzing with emergency personnel when they arrived – and the paramedics were already packing up their ambulance to go back to their base. It was clear they could be of no use to the victim. A dog van was parked furthest away from the action, its back doors open and two Alsatians lying patiently in the dog cages inside, watching the scene before them. Their original remit, to see if they could find the mysterious wolfman, now superseded.

Forensics were rushing to and fro, putting down walking plates to protect footprint and tyre print evidence. A couple of them were heading into the trees with what looked like a forensic tent to erect over the body: the threat of rain was ever constant.

There was only one public vehicle in the car park, a battered silver Ford Fiesta which looked like it wouldn't pass its next MOT – and had two stickers on the back window. One said *Trees are for Life Save our Forests*. And another was of a Viking in a helmet brandishing a hammer.

As DI Painter got out of the car, a middle-aged woman in white overalls spotted him and walked over.

'Tony,' she greeted him. 'White Caucasian female, about thirty years of age. Defensive wounds, but she was dragged into the trees and strangled, before having symbols carved into her.'

'Any sign of sexual assault?'

'Not that we can see at present. Her bottom clothing hasn't been disturbed, and she's lying on her front. The symbols are on her back. Just give us another five minutes and then I'll get you in to take a look.'

'Thanks, Rachel.'

Overhearing the exchange, Harrison was somewhat relieved that they had a few minutes breathing in the fresh air after the weaving in and out of cars to get here. Viewing a victim's mortal remains was never a particularly pleasant experience at the best of times, but if you were already feeling queasy, it could end up messy. From the looks on DS Reid and DC Gorman's faces, they felt the same.

While they waited, Harrison walked around the car park, searching the ground, and looking at tyre tracks. He ended up at the section where they'd cordoned off an area. A forensic officer was taking photographs and preparing to take casts of the tyre tracks, while another worked on the footprints.

'We're not certain these are related, but they're the freshest tracks besides those of the dog team,' the young man said to him.

Harrison examined the tracks the man was working on and agreed.

'Do you have an estimate for the time of death yet? It rained in the night, didn't it?'

The young man nodded.

'Pathologist hasn't been, but the boss reckons early this morning. Her clothes were damp, but not damp enough to have been out in the rain. Chucked it down about three or four a.m., so we're thinking it had to be between four and seven. Dog team arrived at eight thirty and she was cold. She's just started to show signs of rigor mortis. These are the only tyre tracks that haven't gathered any rainwater, which is why we're thinking they could belong to the killer.'

Harrison focused on the treads, looking at the size and width.

'A four-by-four by the looks of it.'

'Yeah, I reckon,' the young man agreed.

Harrison followed the footprints from the area around the tyre tracks. If this was the killer's, then he needed to see how the attack had panned out. It was a man's shoe, like a leather shoe. Not walking-in-the-woods footwear. Beside it, with highly erratic steps, were the prints of a woman's size trainer. Probably a five or six. Harrison could see exactly where she'd struggled with the man. Scuffs in the mud, vegetation on the side of the path crushed. Their killer had virtually dragged her into the trees.

Were her hands tied? Had she kicked at him? Was she gagged so she couldn't scream? Nobody close by to hear if she had. How had he dragged her? By her hair, or was there a rope around her neck as with Dax? It was clear from the tracks that she'd met him in the car park, but had they arranged to meet – and did she know him? Or was it random? Had he attacked her straight away, or had they argued?

'We can go in now.' DC Gorman appeared at Harrison's side. 'The crime scene manager has given us the all clear. We've just got to stick to the stepping plates.'

Harrison let Sally walk on ahead, following the backs of DS Reid and DI Painter. It was important that he continue looking at the story the tracks were telling him. He reclaimed his focus and concentrated on the ground again.

As he walked, he saw the panic and the fight rising in the wearer of the trainers. Her footprints showed where she had struggled to get away, heels digging down into the mud, soles not placed flat or in one direction. At one point, she had broken from her killer's grip and crashed through some tall plants that ran along the path, but she hadn't got far before he had hauled her back. After that, she started to lose strength, feet scuffing the ground. Had he hit her to stop her from fighting? Her footsteps spoke of a distinct shift in her gait from pulling away from him, to stumbling, struggling.

He'd dragged her along with him. Harrison could hear her desperate sobs, feel her fear as they moved further into the dark wood. She would have begged for her life. He was determined. Callous. Like other killers before him, in that moment he was inhuman.

Harrison reached DI Painter, DS Reid, DC Gorman, and the crime scene manager, Rachel, huddled together, their backs to him as they were staring at something on the ground a couple of feet in front of them. This was where she'd met her death. Here on the wet forest floor, amid the mud and leaf mulch, with only the trees to bear witness.

Harrison held back, wanting to get a clear view of the kill site.

DC Sally Gorman turned and saw him. 'Dr Lane! It's Summer. Summer Frances.'

The faceless, terrified woman in his head suddenly had a personality and a voice. An image of Summer looking up at him after she'd read him the runes yesterday came into Harrison's mind. His heart bled for her. Another young life extinguished.

Any residual thoughts of his own troubles disappeared. He needed to find the man who had taken the life of tree-loving Dax and the free spirit of Summer. This man had to face justice.

DI Painter looked over to where Harrison still stood about ten feet from Summer's body.

'Harrison. We'll get out of your way and let you take a look. There's not much room here.'

DI Painter said something to the others, and they all turned and headed towards Harrison along the stepping blocks.

'She was strangled with a rope. Three symbols like Dax,' the DI said to him as he passed.

Harrison gave no reply. He waited for them all to leave and then stepped forward along the plates, continuing the death trail of the victim he now knew was Summer.

A few feet from her body, he saw evidence that she'd regained her strength. Probably knowing she was near to death, she'd fought back with everything she had. Broken foliage and churned ground were witness to the struggle between her and the attacker. Then she was on the ground. She was no match for him. Her fingers had clawed at the earth, presumably as he'd started to strangle the life from her.

Harrison stepped forward to where she had finally come to rest, lying face down on the ground. She was fully clothed on her bottom half, jeans and trainers. Her jacket had been pulled off her and thrown to one side, then her top ripped or cut open in the back. Her hair braid had been pushed up and over the top of her head, half lying on the forest floor. The killer had positioned her like this, pulling the clothes from her upper body and undoing her back bra strap, so that he could carve three rune symbols into her soft, pale skin. Fehu, Uruz, and Thurisaz. The symbols weren't as deeply gouged into the skin as they had been on Dax. It was almost as though he'd gently marked her. Perhaps whatever anger that had driven him to kill her was already spent. Or maybe he had some vestige of a nurturing side of him in his black heart, and cutting a woman had been harder than cutting a man.

Harrison sighed for the young woman who would no longer ride horses or sit on her big red cushion. The knowledge of her last few minutes was painful, but also essential. It would keep him focused, ensure that he did his utmost to find her killer.

Finally, Harrison looked beyond Summer at the surrounding ground.

He saw the big paw prints of the police dog, and the boots of its handler, who must have come to see why it was making a fuss. The officer had clearly followed protocol, stopping as soon as he'd come across Summer, probably bending or crouching down to check for signs of life, and then taking his dog and retreating the same way they had come in order to protect the crime scene. But there were other prints.

Harrison stepped carefully around Summer's body and bent down to look at the ground. The prints were a trainer and man-sized – not Summer's – and underneath the dog paws, so the dogs had come after. He walked as far as the stepping plates allowed him and saw the tracks disappear back into the forest. He didn't want to follow them for fear of losing evidence. Instead, he turned and headed back to find DI Painter, who was deep in conversation with his team and Rachel.

'I don't think it's the same killer,' Harrison interrupted.

'What? Why?' DI Painter asked him, spinning round to face Harrison.

'The symbols are drawn slightly differently, and they're the first three runes. Most of the time when you see a rune table, those will be the first three depicted, so if somebody is going to do a copycat killing, then they're likely to choose those. There's no knowledge involved.'

'How do you mean, they're drawn differently? Because they're on her back?'

'No. It's Thurisaz. On Dax, the killer had drawn it with a sharp point – like a triangular flag half-mast on a pole. On Summer, it's rounded, more like a p.'

'That all? Perhaps they change their writing like we do our handwriting, or maybe they're just not too good at carving into human skin?'

'No. Dax was killed for all to see, his death a symbol in itself. Summer's was hurried and he knew her. Maybe she met him here because she trusted him, or maybe he tricked her. I don't know. But when he positioned her, he gave her some dignity, and he didn't want to look in her eyes, see her face, as he carved the symbols.'

'That doesn't mean the two murders were done by a different killer, just that he knew Summer and didn't know Dax.'

'Possibly, but I don't think so.'

'Mmmh, I don't know. There are lots of similarities. She was strangled with a rope. We've found the murder weapon just off the path. And anyway, we never released the information about the symbols to the public. The only person who knew about what had been done to Dax was the killer, our team, and the dog walker who found him. He promised not to disclose any information and I think he would stick to his word.'

'They must have found out somehow. Perhaps they know the killer. Also, there's something else,' Harrison added. 'Before the dogs arrived, another person found Summer. The four-by-four driver who dragged her from the car park and killed her wore smart shoes. This person wore trainers, and they came from the forest, not the car park.'

'Are you sure? How can you know that?'

'Come with me, I'll show you.'

Harrison walked back to where Summer lay, and all three detectives and the crime scene manager followed him.

'Here, you can see that the dog's paw prints are on top of the trainer prints. They're about a size eight, I'd say. Bigger than Summer's and a different patterned sole. The size of a small man or tall woman. I followed them some way, but if the dogs are still here, maybe we can track them.'

DI Painter was still peering at the ground.

'You're right,' Rachel, the crime scene manager, exclaimed. 'We'd only focused on the footprints leading to her so far. How did you manage to spot those?'

'I started tracking at a young age.'

Rachel looked suitably impressed.

'So, are you thinking that it could be the wolfman? Could he have come across her already dead and then carved the runes onto her?' DI Painter asked. 'Or maybe he's working with somebody?'

'It's a possibility. We have no information about him. He could have copied the symbols like he'd seen on Dax, but I think it's more likely that he just found her as we did,' Harrison replied.

'I'd agree,' Rachel added. 'There aren't enough of his tracks around the body to indicate that he'd spent any length of time there or moved around her.'

'It could have just been a walker out early who got frightened and left. Maybe they heard the dogs coming and thought they'd get blamed.'

Harrison watched DI Painter's face as he worked through the possibilities. He said nothing further, but hoped the DI would come to the conclusion he wanted him to. He did.

'We have to get the dogs back out. If this was wolfman, then we need to find him now – and even if he's not involved in the murders, it looks like he's at least witnessed them both.'

20

Harrison, Painter, Reid, and Gorman were gathered around the two dog handlers.

'It's good conditions for them,' the tall, bearded dog team officer was saying. 'Damp, and shady means the scent will have clung on, and the chill air will keep it low to the ground. Only issue we might come up against is that the dogs have been here a while already and got hyped up by the earlier find. But let's get started and give them a go.'

The two dogs didn't look remotely tired. They jumped out of the van, tails wagging and eyes bright with expectation. DI Painter telephoned Rachel, who had returned to where Summer lay, and told her what they were going to do. They'd start a little way off from the body, where Harrison had seen the tracks disappearing into the woods. That way, they wouldn't interfere with the crime scene while forensics were still working.

'We need to keep back. Let the dogs get a clear scent and let the handlers do their jobs,' DI Painter said to his team. 'We'll follow at a safe distance. I need one of you two to stay here as liaison.' He looked between Reid and Gorman. Sally's face fell.

'I'll stay. Don't fancy traipsing through wet woods anyway,' Freddie said to his boss, and Sally immediately cheered up. 'We've just had confirmation that the silver Fiesta is registered to Summer, so I'll get that picked up,' Freddie continued.

A few minutes later, DI Painter, Harrison, and DC Sally Gorman moved off, walking fast into the trees behind the dog handlers. There was something exciting and yet also primal about it. They needed to track down the wolfman, but hunting a man with dogs smacked of a barbaric heathen practice from centuries gone. It somehow insinuated that their prey was less human. Harrison swallowed his discomfort. He himself tracked people. It was a justifiable means to an end.

Once the dogs had picked up the scent from near to the murder scene, they moved fast, tails wagging, noses to the ground, occasionally barking in excitement. They all strode deeper into the forest, away from the main footpath. Here, the woods started to close in on them, the trees colluding to confuse the eye. No one said a word, everyone focused on the canine hunters who seemed intent on the scent of their prey.

Harrison also kept his eye on the ground. He'd tried to see if they followed the footsteps which led from the crime scene, but at times they were moving so fast it was difficult to keep track.

Occasionally, one of the humans would trip or slip on the wet fallen branches and tree roots. At one point, they suddenly stopped, the dogs running in circles.

'It's possible they might be picking up several trails he's taken. We know he's been seen several times, so it's inevitable that his scent will be in more than one direction,' one of the handlers said to them.

The dogs seemed to make a decision and their entourage were all off again, stomping through the undergrowth, their eyes open for any glimpses of wolfman among the trees. At one point, they crossed the main pathway that ran from the car park to the clearing with the yew, but didn't follow it. Instead, the dogs plunged into the trees again, their small posse of five humans crashing after them.

They continued weaving amongst the trees until Harrison detected that they were getting close to the edge of the forest. It was getting lighter, more undergrowth and the trees were further apart and younger. As the forest came to an end and a field lay in front of them, he realised where they were.

DI Painter voiced it. 'That's where Dax's caravan is. Wilson Johnson's place.'

The dogs were in full pelt now, spurring their handlers on across the field, straight for the small caravan site. DI Painter was on his radio, breathlessly speaking to DS Reid and asking for some backup.

Wilson Johnson must have seen and heard them coming because as they broke through a gap in the hedging and arrived in amongst the caravans, he appeared at the entrance to the site.

'What's going on?' he shouted.

'Police, Mr Johnson. We're tracking someone,' DI Painter replied, then added in a quieter voice, 'Sally, can you go and tell him to get back inside and I'll come and talk to him in a bit?'

'Sir.' She nodded and walked over to the old man, putting a hand on his back, and guiding him out of the site field.

The dogs stood barking outside Dax's caravan. One of them had mounted the metal steps and was scratching at the door, whining.

'Right. Is there any other way out?' DI Painter asked Harrison and the two handlers.

'Windows either side, but if we're at the front here we can see if anyone tries to exit. There's no window at the back,' Harrison replied.

'Good. What do you want to do?' Painter asked the dog handlers now.

'I don't want to send the dogs in if he's in there ready for them with a knife,' the bearded handler replied.

'No. Agreed. How likely is it that he is in there?'

'No guarantees. I can definitely say he's been here, but we can't be one hundred per cent certain he's still in there.'

'OK, call the dogs back.' DI Painter's face hardened, and he walked across to the caravan and up the steps, knocking on the door.

'Police. Show yourself. Come outside with your hands where we can see them.' He paused a moment, listening and watching. 'We know you're in there and we'll send in the dogs if you don't come out immediately.'

Everyone waited. The dogs, tired after their full morning's work, sat on their haunches and stared at the caravan with their tongues out, panting.

'Could he be in one of the other vans?' DI Painter asked the dog handlers.

'I'll take Rocket and do a sweep,' the other handler said, calling his dog to his side and walking towards the nearest caravan.

Harrison was on full alert, his eyes constantly scanning in case the man came out from somewhere they weren't expecting.

DI Painter knocked again.

'This is your last warning. If you don't come out of the caravan immediately, with your hands where we can see them, then we're coming in.'

The three remaining men stared at the caravan door.

It stayed closed.

'Right, we've no reason to think he has a firearm, so stand back, I'm opening the door,' DI Painter said to Harrison and the dog handler.

He pulled the door open and jumped back down the steps, just in case somebody lunged at him from the doorway.

Nothing.

'Would the dog tell us if he's still in there?' Painter asked the handler.

'Let's see.' The bearded man stepped forward, his dog on a tight leash. The animal was barking excitedly, picking up on the adrenaline of those around him. DI Painter backed away from the snapping jaws, allowing the dog to bound towards the van. He put his nose to the ground, and on the steps, but once he reached the doorway, there was no uptick in his excitement. No increase in his barking and tail wagging to show the dog thought he'd found their prey.

'I think he's gone.'

'Bloody hell,' DI Painter said.

The handler went up the steps and cautiously peered into the van. Then he let the dog off its leash, reassured that there wasn't an unwelcome reception for him inside. The dog shot in, clearly still following the scent, and the handler followed behind. A short while later, DI Painter joined them. Harrison stayed outside, watching in case the man had been hiding and suddenly broke cover.

'Nothing,' Painter said, coming back down the caravan steps. 'He's gone, but the cupboard doors were open. Whatever measly supplies that Dax had are now missing. He's nicked the lot. We'll get the place dusted for prints.'

At the same time, the other dog handler returned with Rocket.

'No indications in any of the other vans,' he reported back.

Tony Painter rubbed at his head with both his palms. 'Bloody hell. Thought we had him. OK, thanks, lads.'

Painter sat down on one of the rickety chairs around the BBQ area, his elbows on his knees. 'I'll get someone to drive your dog van over and come pick us up,' he said to them. 'Forensics can dust the caravan, but I think we're done here for today.' He looked up at them, tiredness in his red-ringed eyes.

The disappointment was felt by them all. The expectation of

the chase had brought with it hopes that they might possibly get some answers about their murderer and solve the legend of the wolfman. The sound of a siren approaching told them that their backup had just arrived. It was another wasted journey.

21

———

He'd heard them. The dogs baying for his blood. Searching for him. It wasn't the first time he'd been hunted like that. The sound brought back the memories, the fear. The bad spirits which haunted every waking and sleeping hour.

He had been lucky this time. They'd not tracked him back to his hiding place, but it had been close, and they might come back.

He'd become careless, more reckless even. That didn't serve well in his position.

It was time to move on. There was nothing left for him here. Just like before.

But this time, his soul was empty. The past week had drained from him the last vestiges of his humanity. It had also drained his hope. He was just a husk, surviving, but for what? He wasn't sure how much he had left to keep fighting.

22

—————

DI Painter sent Reid and Gorman back to the incident room so they could brief the rest of the team and chase up some of the most pressing leads. Everyone but Painter and Harrison had left the Johnson caravan site. A slight mist had started to descend across the field, giving the place an other worldly feel; as though something or somebody they were least expecting might suddenly appear through the grey wispy haze. Harrison stood with his back to the campsite, looking towards the trees. Goose-bumps tingled on his upper arms, and he felt the hairs prick on the back of his neck. It was a scene that had probably changed little over the centuries; the fields might have become more regular with their hedging and gates, and the forest matured, but he could almost imagine the Vikings striding across, their families following as they visited their sacred grove in the trees.

For a moment, Harrison thought he saw movement. On the edge of the forest, a shadow. He strained to see and then smiled as a small family of deer cautiously stepped into the open. He let out a big sigh. The peace of nature, a respite that he'd needed.

Two officers arrived with Painter's car, driven over from the car park for them as the detective had refused to walk another yard. Harrison got into the front passenger seat. They'd had to wait a few moments before driving off to clear the windscreen. The pair of them were still warm after the race across the forest and had instantly fogged up the car.

'I was going to suggest we take a quick pit stop and grab a bite to eat as I'm bloody starving,' Painter said to Harrison, 'but Dr Bannister has just called to say she's finished with Dax. While I might have been in Serious Crime for more years than I care to remember, I still can't get used to the stench of death and sight of a human body cut open. If you don't mind, can we wait for refreshments until after we've visited the morgue?'

'That's fine. I'm fasting today anyway, so it would just be water for me.'

'Fasting! Bloody hell, are you a saint?' Painter twisted round in his seat to look at the muscular man beside him. 'You young men these days. You won't get to grow up and have my fine physique unless you eat a few pies, you know.' DI Painter jokingly pushed his stomach out and patted it.

Harrison smiled appreciatively at the attempt to lighten the mood. It had been a hard morning already and the prospect of being reacquainted with Dax was not one either of them would be looking forward to.

The morgue was buried in a large hospital complex, which they eventually managed to reach after negotiating a complex network of car parks that all seemed to be frustratingly full.

'You met Dr Christine Bannister that first morning. Very professional, but not a woman you argue with,' DI Painter said to Harrison as they approached the entrance to the morgue.

Harrison got the impression that she and Tony had some kind of previous. It might explain why he'd not stepped in to aid Freddie on that first morning. Too afraid of getting caught in the crossfire, or perhaps he wanted to let Freddie get the dressing down he needed. The young detective had been less ebullient with his jokes since then. DI Painter himself had said he over-stepped the mark, and it sounded as if a woman like Dr Bannister was just the person to shove him right back over it.

The morgue door was opened by a middle-aged woman, whose ID badge said *Magda Bielawski*. DI Painter showed her his ID and said he was there to see Dr Bannister.

Magda didn't let them in through the door immediately and Harrison was just wondering what the reason for her reticence might be when he followed her raised eyebrows and gazed down to their feet. DI Painter also cottoned on at the same time. Both of them had mud covered shoes.

'Ah!' he said. 'Apologies. We've just come from a crime scene.'

'I will find you some alternative shoes,' Magda said in a light Polish accent. 'Your sizes, please?'

'Ten for me,' DI Painter said.

'Twelve,' Harrison replied.

'Stay here, please.'

She allowed them to stand inside the door and disappeared off to find them each a pair of rubber ankle boots, which were often used by the mortuary staff to protect their feet from the various fluids that might be produced, or to wash the floors down. The corridor they were stood in was familiar to Harrison. He'd been to many mortuaries like this one in his career. The strip lighting, the clinical walls, the smell of chemicals which didn't always succeed in covering the stench of death.

'Sorry, the biggest we have is just eleven.' Magda appeared from a door to the left and walked towards them, brandishing two pairs of boots. She handed Harrison his with an apologetic smile.

'I'll manage,' he replied, bracing himself to spend the next forty-five minutes with his toes scrunched up against the front of the unforgiving rubber.

Once she was happy that they weren't going to contaminate or dirty the examination areas, Magda showed them through to where Dr Bannister was standing at a desk, writing some notes.

'DI Painter.' She tipped her head to him. 'And we weren't introduced.' She looked to Harrison.

'Dr Harrison Lane, head of the Ritualistic Behavioural Crime unit.'

'Dr Lane has been sent by the National Crime Agency to help us with the symbols and ritualistic nature of our victim's murder.'

'Victims, I hear now?' Dr Bannister corrected, emphasising the plural.

'Yes. Unfortunately, you will shortly be receiving a female who was found this morning in the same woods. Forensics should give the go-ahead to move her sometime later this morning.'

'We'd better crack on then with our current resident, Mr Moore,' Dr Bannister said, walking off towards an examination room.

Dax Moore's mortal remains were lying like a wax effigy on the steel examination table. Harrison certainly didn't enjoy this part of his job, but his mind was able to detach itself from the experience because he always felt as though the bodies were just the spent husks of the people that once lived in them. It was a strange concept for the spiritual sceptic, but he felt that the energy of life most definitely left its earthly remains at the end. Harrison was a man of fact and science, so he rationalised it as a physical effect. He could understand why others believed differently. That a person's conscience, thoughts, personality, and experiences couldn't just simply be erased by the stopping of a heart. He hadn't known Dax in life – like with so many of his victims, he was acquainted only with their physical remains, but he never forgot that they had once been human beings full of life, love, and hope.

'We've mostly used scans, as the cause of death was so obvious,' Dr Bannister interrupted his thoughts. 'I remember that you asked me if he was speared before or after death. I believe it was before, although only shortly before. There was some considerable force behind it and it was angled from a higher height than you would expect from an attacker on the ground. I know that horse hoof prints were found at the clearing and that to me would fit with the likelihood that someone ran at him on horseback and speared him as he stood there.'

'Bloody hell,' DI Painter exclaimed.

'Indeed,' Dr Bannister continued. 'After incapacitating him with the spear, I'd guess that's when he put the noose around his neck and hung him. As I said before, the spear wouldn't have killed him, at least not quickly, but he'd have been floored by it.'

Harrison looked at the entrance wound for the spear and thought about how the shock alone would have meant Dax was unlikely to be able to defend himself.

'The most interesting finding, which wasn't so obvious,' Dr Bannister continued, 'was that he'd been in a fight quite recently. His beard and long hair had hidden the injuries.'

Harrison peered at the newly shaven face of Dax Moore. It made him look younger than Harrison had initially thought, a common result of someone shaving off a beard. On his jaw was a clear bruise, with a further bruise around his right eye socket.

'There's also some bruising in his rib area, but he gave back as good as he got, if the grazing on his knuckles is anything to go by.'

'Can you say when he received these injuries?' DI Painter asked.

Harrison knew full well what he was thinking.

'I'd say probably the Friday, or possibly the Thursday. The bruising had all come out well before death.'

'Interesting, thank you,' DI Painter replied.

'I suppose you want to know as much as possible about the symbols, Dr Lane?' Dr Bannister looked at him.

'They look to me as though they were cut deeply in anger,' he said to her.

'Yes. I'd say you're right. They weren't just surface scratches, that's for sure. He really carved them into him using some force and they were inflicted before death.'

'Before death?' DI Painter's eyes widened.

'Yes. Not a great deal of time before, but definitely before. Probably as Dax was lying on the ground following the spear attack. While incapacitated, they carved the symbols on him and then hung him.'

'There's definitely signs of a struggle around the tree, as though he resisted being hung,' Harrison said to her, thinking through the potential scenario.

'It's more than possible that the pain of having the symbols carved into his skin would have brought him round from the shock of being speared and with the noose around his neck he knew he'd be fighting for his life.'

'Anything underneath the fingernails or any hope of the attacker's DNA on him anywhere?' DI Painter asked.

'I've not found anything obvious yet, but we've sent everything off to the lab. His hands were heavily soiled from the forest floor so it was difficult to see if there was any potential trace evidence mixed in.'

'You're saying "he" – are you definitely sure that it was a male who did this?' DI Painter asked.

'Tony, as you're well aware, we can't be definite about anything, but from what I saw at the scene and the nature of the crime, I'd say it was more likely to be a male. A proficient horsewoman might have been able to do it because the killer obviously used the strength of the horse to pull him up the tree. If she'd anchored the rope correctly, then it's quite feasible that she would have managed even when he fought back. But to spear him like this, she'd have probably been knocked off the horse, unless she was used to that kind of action. I'm sure Dr Lane would also have more to say about the likelihood of this being a woman.'

'I agree with you, Dr Bannister. Physically, it's difficult to see how a woman could have done this, even with the help of the horse, and the violence used is not typical of women. As we all know, females account for just five per cent of the offenders in our prisons and only a tiny percentage of those are for violent crimes. Whoever did this to Dax harboured a great deal of anger and resentment. It would be highly unusual for a woman to run someone down and spear them, carve symbols into their flesh, and then hang them. I'm not saying it's impossible, but I believe a man did this. Somebody who was very angry with Dax, for deep, personal reasons. It was a punishment, retribution. Perhaps they had felt that anger towards him for a while, but something triggered this. Critically, they didn't lose control. Whoever it is has a great deal of discipline. They planned it carefully, and the anger was very focused.'

'But why the Viking stuff?'

'I think that the symbols are a well-thought-out statement by the killer who clearly has some knowledge of these things,' Harrison replied.

'So, we need to speak to Patrick as a matter of urgency if we think it's nothing to do with Summer,' the DI said to him.

'I'm not saying that it's nothing to do with Summer. It's still possible that she may have introduced the killer to this, encouraged it, not realising that he would turn it into something deadly. There are some who revere the Vikings because of their tales of violence. They only see the terrifying invaders who came and took what they wanted and that can feed into those with a personality dominated by toxic masculinity.'

The three of them stood there in silence for a few moments, looking at the sad result of one man's anger.

'Right. Thank you, Dr Bannister. We had better get on with hunting this man down, unless there's anything else you think we need to know?' DI Painter asked.

'Actually, yes, there is something. It's related to his lifestyle rather than his death, but it might help with your enquiries. Dax Moore was homosexual, and he was in an active relationship.'

23

'Bloody hell,' DI Painter said as they walked down the corridor from the morgue.

Harrison was fast coming to realise that *bloody hell* was Painter's favourite expression.

'I had Dax and Summer down as a couple, despite what she'd said. Now we've got to find his boyfriend which could open this up to a whole new community and motive. But then where does Summer fit in? Unless Dax swung both ways?'

'Always possible, but maybe they were just friends and co-protestors.'

'Well let's get straight round to her house and see what we can find. We need to work out why she ended up in those woods so early in the morning. She had to be meeting someone she knew. Surely no woman would be foolish enough to meet a stranger in the darkness in remote woodland?'

'I agree.'

'Then we need to go and see Patrick Sheldon. I'm going to get the team to speak to the gay community and see if they know anything. If there's a gay Viking fanatic out there, then they might know who he is, or at least who Dax might have been seeing. This case gets more complicated by the minute and my retirement clock is ticking.'

Harrison and DI Painter drove to Summer's house and sat in his car, just up the road, while he called into the office. Judging from the scowls and sighs that he was emitting, there wasn't much in the way of good news.

'Summer didn't have her house keys or anything on her. I'll have to get a team dispatched to get us in.'

'Might be worth trying the door anyway, just in case it's not locked,' Harrison offered. 'When we left yesterday, I noticed that the door and the lock were old and quite basic. It's one of those you have to lock once you're outside. It doesn't lock automatically.'

'That would be convenient. You go ahead and be my guest. I've just got to talk to Freddie about pulling Sam Green in. There's no way that he's told us the truth about the fight, and he was friends with both victims.'

Harrison walked up to the little terraced house where he'd met Summer Frances just yesterday. He felt a weight of sadness to now be entering her home, knowing that she would never again breathe its air. Before he grabbed the handle, he put his sleeve over his hand to prevent his fingerprints from transferring. If there was any chance that the killer had pulled the door shut, then he didn't want to destroy the evidence.

The handle turned. He pushed, and the door swung open.

Harrison turned to see if DI Painter had followed him yet. He saw him leaning against the boot of his car, deep in conversation on his phone. Harrison waved and immediately caught his eye.

DI Painter's face registered surprise, but he quickly ended his phone call and took something out of the boot of his car. Harrison guessed it would be some forensic overshoes and gloves.

'You're a genius,' Painter said as he arrived at the front door, a little out of breath.

They put on the overshoes and gloves and stepped inside the narrow entrance hall. This time there was no Summer to show them into the sitting room. The air was still, the house already in mourning.

DI Painter poked his head around the sitting-room door and looked.

'I'll do a quick check around, see if there're any signs of a struggle. We've got no guarantee that she drove her car to those woods herself. See what you can find.'

He disappeared up the hall into the tiny kitchen at the end.

Harrison walked into the living room which still contained the echo of its owner, taking the time to look at the details and not just the overall picture. The first thing he noticed was that there was a distinct smell of cleaning spray. All the surfaces seemed to have been wiped and dusted. The second thing was that the Valentine's card had gone.

He walked across to the bookcase to see if the card could have fallen or if Summer had taken it down to look at. It was nowhere in sight. The room was small, there were barely any possible hiding places, so he searched everywhere, flicking through every book, underneath the big red cushion and bean-bags, even behind the posters on the wall. He opened the pouch with her runes inside and took another look at them. He had been right. Her Thurisaz was pointed.

'Found anything?' DI Painter walked into the room as Harrison had just finished poking through the ash in the fire grate – just in case.

'The Valentine's card has gone. Did you see it upstairs or in the kitchen?'

'No. But I wasn't looking specifically for that. I'll go check the bins.'

Harrison followed the DI into the kitchen and watched as he

looked through the small plastic bin. It was clearly not there. He peered out of the back door into the garden. It was a tiny concrete yard, no more than ten or twelve feet in length, surrounded by an ageing wooden fence with a gate at the end.

'There's a small green wheelie bin out there. I'll go check that. You keep looking.' DI Painter went to unlock the back door. 'This door's unlocked, too. I'll take a look where that gate leads.'

Harrison searched through the cupboards and the fridge. Checked the drawers and even the pockets of the coats, which were hanging up on a large hook in the corner. Nothing. He made his way upstairs as he saw DI Painter disappearing through the wooden gate at the end of the garden.

The upstairs consisted of one bedroom, plus a tiny bathroom with toilet and an even tinier second bedroom that could only just fit a single bed. Summer had obviously not been able to afford a spare bed, but there was a mattress on the floor, presumably for when friends stayed over. He lifted the mattress, checking underneath for anything that could shed some light on what had happened, as well as where the card had gone. All he found was a biro pen and a KitKat wrapper.

The bathroom was illuminating. Not for what he found, but more for what he didn't find. It was the same in Summer's bedroom. Her bed had been stripped of bedclothes and pillows. Harrison's heart sank. The killer had clearly removed anything they thought could tie them to their victim and cleaned up any possibility of fingerprints. He was unlikely to find anything, but he'd look anyway. They'd need forensics to do a thorough search. If the killer had been a regular visitor, then there was a strong chance just dusting and hoovering wouldn't have erased all traces of them.

Harrison looked through the wardrobes, checking every pocket, every drawer. He lifted up the mattress, peered underneath the bed, rifled through the small cabinet by the bedside, and looked in the pots and boxes on her windowsill and the small dressing table. Finally, he checked the clothes thrown over the back of the chair. He recognised them as what she'd been wearing yesterday when they'd interviewed her. Harrison felt something in the jeans' pocket. It was a plastic card, credit card sized and a folded piece of paper.

'Nothing out there but the gate leads to a quiet back road. If I was the killer, that's where I'd have parked so nobody saw me. What you got?' DI Painter walked into the room.

'It's a library card.'

'Uh. OK. You looked everywhere else? I reckon he's not only stripped the bed but also hoovered and wiped. Of course, she could have been doing some cleaning.'

'No, it was him. He's taken the pillows. They'd still be on the bed if Summer was doing washing, and we'd have seen the sheets downstairs in the washing machine. Also, there's no toothbrush in the bathroom. I think he's taken that, too, for fear of there being any DNA evidence on it.'

'Yeah, you're right. Which means whoever her killer is, he was having a relationship with Summer, and a sexual one if he was sleeping in her bed. I'll mention that to Dr Bannister. If we're really lucky, we might find some trace evidence of him on Summer.'

'Yes, but this library card is significant. I think we have our first strong lead.'

DI Painter looked at him as though he was mad.

'What's so significant about that?'

'Yesterday, she told us that the day Dax died, he had gone to the library. Then, the minute we leave here, she goes to the library, too. This is a leaflet they give to all new library users so it was clearly her first visit.' Harrison held up the folded piece of paper. 'She was at work in the morning, so it could only have been after we left that she went. So, why the dash to the library, unless she thought Dax had found something which might have resulted in his death?'

'You could be onto something, although what on earth would he find at a library that means two people had to die?'

Harrison shrugged and DI Painter sighed.

'I want to go and see our Viking friend, Patrick Sheldon. See what he has to say about everything. Find out if he's going to be as cagey as Sam Green, or if we might finally start getting some answers.'

24

Patrick Sheldon's house was on a local authority estate in a cul-de-sac of 1970s build homes, where the front gardens displayed the personalities of their occupants. His contained an old motorbike, definitely not roadworthy, along with several random parts seemingly abandoned by the side of the path. Out front was parked an old Land Rover. Next door was clearly a family home with a kid's tricycle on the small patch of lawn, and what looked like a plastic hoe and trowel where the small human had obviously been attempting some gardening. On the other side, heavy metal music could be heard pounding through the bedroom window. Not loud enough to be a real nuisance, but just enough to provide an irritating background thump.

Patrick's house was otherwise unremarkable, certainly no evidence of an obsession with Vikings on the outside. DI Painter pressed the doorbell, which emitted a buzzing ring somewhere in the hallway. He also used the door knocker for good measure. Heavy footsteps preceded a tall, broad outline through the frosted glass of the door. DI Painter took a step back, clearly aware that the man who was about to open the door was somewhat larger and more powerful than himself.

Patrick opened the door and stood staring at them aggressively. 'What now?' he said. 'What you come to harass me about?'

He was tall and broad, muscular, with thick arms. He had a full head of hair that reached to his shoulders and a big beard and moustache. Harrison suspected that the tattoo which peered above his sweatshirt collar was probably just one of many on his body. He was a man who prided himself on looking tough, and had clearly had dealings with the law before, which was why he'd been able to instantly tell they were police.

'Patrick Sheldon?' DI Painter asked.

'That's me, but I presume you know that, seeing as you're knocking on my door.'

'DI Painter and Dr Harrison Lane. We wondered if we could come in and ask you a few questions.'

'About what?'

'About Dax Moore. I presume you know that Dax was found murdered two days ago? We're talking to anyone who knew him to see if we can get some idea of Dax's movements.'

Patrick seemed to think for a moment before grunting, stepping out of blocking the doorway and backing into his hall. They took that as a yes and an invitation to follow him inside.

He led them into an ordinary looking sitting room with a faux leather couch and armchair, a large flat-screen TV, and a cat scratch tower near the patio doors that looked out onto a small, decked area and lawn.

'You live alone?' DI Painter asked nonchalantly.

'No. My partner Alison lives here, too.'

'You were in the army before?'

'Yeah. Been out a while now.'

'Mr Sheldon, I understand you were also a friend of Summer Frances?'

'Were?' Patrick didn't miss the tense change and his attitude suddenly altered. Concern replaced any lingering signs of indifference.

'Yes. I'm sorry to tell you that Ms Frances was found dead this morning.'

'Shit.' Patrick collapsed down onto the sofa. 'What the hell happened to her?'

'We believe she was also murdered.'

'Why? That's just crazy. Why would anyone want to kill Summer, or Dax?' Patrick looked from Painter to Harrison.

'We don't know yet and we're hoping you can help us to work that out.'

Patrick bent his head into both his hands, leaning his elbows on his knees.

'I don't know.'

Painter gave him a few moments.

'When was the last time you saw Dax?'

'Last week. Wednesday, I think. I met him in the pub for a pint. He was trying to get some more work. There's not much call for forest bathing in the winter and he needed money. He wondered if I knew of anything.'

'And did you?'

'Just the usual suggestions. Told him there was an agency in town that was always looking for casual labour, or he should try the pubs and restaurants. They're desperate for staff at the moment.'

'How did he seem to you?'

'Fine.'

'He didn't express any other concerns or seem worried about anything?'

'No. I'd say he's got a bit quieter lately. Not been going to as many protests. I thought maybe he'd met someone.'

'Any idea who?'

Patrick shook his head.

'How about Summer? Do you know if she was seeing someone?'

'Summer always seemed to have a guy around. She was a pretty girl and lived life on her own terms. I wasn't aware of anyone in particular. Certainly nobody that she'd introduced to us.'

'What about her and Dax?'

'They were close, but they always denied anything other than friends.'

'What was your relationship with Summer like?'

'Me? If you're asking was I shagging Summer, then the answer is no. I'm happy with my Alison. She'd cut my balls off anyway if I was unfaithful.'

'I was meaning how close were you, platonically?'

'We were mates. Shared common interests.'

'When was the last time you saw Summer?'

'Probably about a week or so ago. Weekend before last, I think. She was the same as usual. Read me the runes and we talked about her joining our re-enactment group.'

'Is that you?' DI Painter asked, pointing to a photograph on the wall of a Viking battle scene with Patrick at the front of the fighting. He was riding a horse, sword raised.

'Yeah. That's for one of the Netflix series. I've also done documentaries and we do local re-enactments for history events.'

'You're a proficient horseman, then?'

'Good enough. My cousins had ponies when I was a kid and they used to let me ride them.'

'What got you interested in the re-enactment scene?'

'Just always been interested in Vikings, ever since I read about them at school. Kind of fell into it after I left the army. It's not easy for everyone coming out of the services. Officers have their networks which help them with management and leadership roles, but us foot soldiers, we're not so sought after. Sometimes it's downright negative. I've met idiots who think I'm bound to be some headcase who likes shooting people, or else suffering from PTSD. An old mate introduced me to the re-enactment group. It gave me another team to be a part of.'

'You're also in the Ragnarok eco group, too?'

'Yeah!'

'Do you go to protests a lot?'

'That's the other thing about the army. You get to see and take part in a lot of destruction, so now I want to protect. Protect the environment and the trees. I'd still like to have kids one day. There's going to be nothing left for them soon. The Vikings thought many trees were sacred and they are, they help our planet. The trees can't speak for themselves, so I do it for them.'

'Not always legally, though.' Painter raised an eyebrow at him.

Patrick's face clouded over and some of the old animosity seemed to return. He didn't say anything.

'Has Ragnarok created any enemies? Perhaps someone or an organisation who might not have taken kindly to your protests?'

'We're protesting. We're not trying to win a popularity contest.'

'I appreciate that fact, Mr Sheldon, but we're looking for somebody who might have decided to get back at Dax.'

Patrick shook his head. 'No.'

'You sure? Nothing planned that someone could have got wind of?'

Patrick shook his head and looked at Painter under his eyebrows, but Harrison detected a slight hesitation in his answer.

'You work?' Painter changed the subject.

'Yeah, waste operative.' He looked at DI Painter's nonplussed face. 'Bin man.'

'Early shifts then, yeah?'

'Yeah.'

'Are all the others in the group as into Vikings as you?'

Harrison asked him now and Patrick turned his gaze towards him as though assessing him.

'Summer is, Dax from the trees point of view. Sam just cares about stopping the rich from getting everything they want and wrecking the environment for everyone, and Steve wants to stop global warming for his kids.'

'I'd have thought you'd have a bit more Viking gear around the place.' Harrison smiled. Fishing.

'Yeah, well, I would if I lived alone, but Alison ain't so keen on having the place look like a Viking longhouse. She lets me keep it all in one room. It's my man cave.'

'I'd love to see, if you wouldn't mind showing us?' Harrison asked. 'I've always been fascinated in the period myself. I'm sure there's plenty of Viking blood in my veins.'

Patrick thought for a moment and then clearly his pride in his 'man cave' won and he decided there was no harm. 'Sure. Why not?'

He led them out of the sitting room and to the other side of the hallway. In other houses it was probably the dining room, or a kids' playroom. In Patrick's house, it was an homage to Vikings. The room had been decorated with wallpaper that looked like wooden panelling. On one wall was a boar's head and on either side of it was a sword and an axe. On the floor and elsewhere on the wall were furs and animal skins. A wooden shield, painted with a yellow background and red and blue triangles, also adorned the wall and in the corner was a wooden bar area with a sign saying Odin's Bar, and an array of spirits along the shelves behind it.

'It's where me and the boys hang out,' Patrick said proudly.

'Impressive,' DI Painter said. 'Where did you get the boar's head?'

'Got that at an auction. Came out of a hotel that was closing down.'

'What about the runes?' Harrison asked. 'I believe Summer used to read the runes. Is that something you do?'

'Not like Summer, no. I know about them, but she is more into the spiritual side than me.' Patrick's face changed to pensive again, and he corrected himself. 'Was.'

'Pretty impressive weapons.' Painter nodded at the axe and sword on the wall. 'Are those what you use for re-enactments?'

'Not those, no. The aim isn't to kill each other. Those are the real McCoy.'

'I'm going to have to ask you where you were on Saturday evening, and also again early this morning?'

'Wondered when we were going to get round to that! Well, it's easy.' Patrick looked smug. 'I was on shift this morning and on Saturday at home here with Alison.'

'Anybody else see you here?'

'No. But Alison will tell you. She's a schoolteacher, so a bit more respectable than me.' He said the latter with some sarcasm, his underlying dislike of the law once again surfacing.

They left shortly after, but not before Harrison had noticed the candles with runes carved into the side of them, and the two knifes in leather sheaths that were behind the bar. He pitied anyone brave enough to try to break into Patrick's house. Question was, did Patrick use them outside his home or were they really just there for decoration?

25

Patrick was glad he'd been forewarned about their visit, and he reckoned he'd pulled it off. Maybe he should be an actor, not just a re-enactor. He'd watched them as they left. They didn't seem to clock his Land Rover or show any interest. He'd been sure that had been caught on a camera. They were going to have to be more careful. For all he knew they might even have them under surveillance. The gear was all well-hidden, everything cleared out of his house the minute he'd had the phone call. They'd got one more job planned and then maybe they'd lie low for a while until the police got bored.

It would be a frustrating but temporary hiccup in their plans. The fight would go on. He relaxed back into the furs on the sofa and closed his eyes. The faces of Dax and Summer came into his head. He pushed them away. He'd never been good at facing up to things.

26

When DI Painter and Harrison arrived back at the station, Sam Green had already been brought in for questioning. Painter had decided he and DS Reid would conduct the interview, while Harrison watched on video feed, with DC Gorman sitting in with Harrison. The young DC was keen to improve her interview technique, and Harrison respected her enthusiasm. The two of them settled down in a room just along the corridor from where the interview was going to take place. Harrison was keen to see how Sam Green reacted now that he was away from his own home turf.

Harrison watched as Sam sloped into the interview room, sullen and defiant looking. His counsel was a young man in his early thirties, nicely suited and presented, and clearly with the ambition to go further in law. He'd spent an hour with Sam prior to the interview, which ran the risk that this time they talked to him, they were more than likely to receive a frustrating succession of 'no comments'.

Once everyone had been introduced and the recording began, Sam lounged back in his chair, putting his arms around the back and opening up his body as if to signal contempt for the process, and that he wasn't in the least bit concerned.

'Are you aware that we found the body of Summer Frances this morning?' DI Painter said to him.

Harrison could see Painter wanted to test Sam before he became entrenched with the line of questions. He got his reaction.

Sam brought his arms forward and scrunched his body inwards, defensively, bending his head.

'Yeah. That's a right shocker, that is,' he said to the floor. 'She was a nice girl.'

Sam looked thoughtful, and the DI gave him a moment to contemplate.

'You got any idea who might have killed her?' he asked.

In response, Sam squeezed his lips together and rumpled his chin, then shook his head.

'This isn't our first conversation. We visited you yesterday to talk through where you were on the night of Dax's murder. Do you recall that?'

'Yeah,' Sam replied, his defensiveness and contempt return- ing. 'I've not got dementia.'

'I wanted to ask you again about the injuries you've sustained to your face and knuckles,' DI Painter continued, ignoring the flippant comment. 'You have bruising that is consistent with having been in a fight and you told us that you had been jumped by three men who beat you up after you left the pub last Friday. I'd like to ask you again if that was what happened?'

'No comment,' Sam replied, glancing at his lawyer.

They'd clearly already discussed how Sam should proceed if the fight was brought up – and Harrison imagined their tactic was probably to find out what the police knew before Sam said anything further.

DI Painter opened a cardboard folder on the desk and took

out two photographs: close-ups of Dax's face, post mortem, shaven and with the bruising clearly visible.

'Dax Moore also has bruises like yours, which the pathologist estimates were likely sustained at the same time as yours were. In addition, while we've managed to confirm that you did indeed visit the Dog and Ball, nobody saw a fight outside. In fact, someone said they saw you ride off on your bike.'

Sam shrugged.

'We are getting the bruises analysed and measured. We think that we'll find the marks on Dax's face fit your fist. We are also gathering various CCTV recordings from your route home and outside your flat.'

Harrison watched Sam's lips roll in and his brows come down, a sign he was getting angry. He glanced at his solicitor, who nodded.

'OK. Yeah, it was Dax I had the fight with. Things just got a bit heated, that's all. Nothing major. He was fine afterwards.'

'So why didn't you tell us this before? Why lie?'

Sam sat up straight and slapped his palms down on the table.

'You're having a laugh, right?' He looked from DI Painter to DS Reid. 'My mate's just been murdered, the geezer I've just had a bust up with the day before. I knew exactly what you were going to think. You were going to try to collar me for it.'

'Did you kill Dax Moore?'

'No, I did not,' Sam replied forcefully and flung himself back in the chair. 'A knock around is one thing, but he was my mate. We'd have made it up over a few beers.'

Harrison saw his eyes go back to the photograph of his friend on the table. Sam shook his head and his lips rolled in again, angry.

'If it wasn't you, then who would have done this? Two of your friends have now been murdered. Chances are you might know the individual who's done this to them.'

Sam shook his head.

'I've no idea.'

'What was the argument with Dax about?'

'No comment.'

'Surely if it was just a friendly tiff, then you won't mind telling us what it was?'

'No comment.'

'Did you argue with Dax because you were jealous?'

'Jealous? Of what?'

'Do you know who Dax was seeing? Who else he hung around with and had a relationship with?'

'I told you, I thought him and Summer were an item. They was always together when I saw 'em.'

'What about your relationship with Summer?'

'My relationship? We were mates, that's it.'

'Were you aware that Dax may have been homosexual?'

Sam's face registered genuine surprise.

'Dax, gay? What? No way. No. He never said nothing to me, and I never saw him with any blokes. He was always a bit of a babe magnet in the pub.'

'Can I ask you where you were early this morning between the hours of four a.m. and eight a.m.?'

'In bed. I do late shifts, so I don't exactly get up at sunrise,' Sam replied with a sneer.

'Can anyone verify that?'

'Yeah, ask Taylor Swift. She was in bed next to me.'

'I take it that's a no?' DI Painter pushed.

Sam's solicitor leaned sideways and murmured something in his ear. It seemed to give Sam a new look of defiance.

'What was your relationship with Summer Frances like?' DI Painter continued.

'No comment,' came Sam's reply.

'Were you sleeping with Summer?'

'No. I've told you,' Sam said, anger again flickering in his eyes.

'Did you see Summer yesterday?'

'No.'

'Did Dax come to find you on the Friday?'

'No comment.'

'How did the argument end? Did you threaten Dax? Did he threaten you?'

'No comment.'

Harrison watched the interview intently, studying Sam's body language, listening to what he said and how he said it. Sally sat silently next to him. He could feel that she was bursting to ask questions but hadn't dared to break his concentration. As the succession of 'no comment' answers continued, she plucked up the courage.

'Can you tell when he's lying?' she asked Harrison. 'Does he look to the side or something?'

'It's not quite that straightforward,' he said, keeping his eyes on the screen and Sam Green. 'You can't read people like books, although some so-called non-verbal communications experts will try to tell you otherwise. Personality has an impact on how you read expressions, for one thing. Then there are the psycho-pathic types who will be consciously pulling certain facial expressions or displaying body language to fool you. They learn those expressions by mirroring others and working out when it's appropriate to use them. Culture also has an impact. To work out what someone like Sam Green's gestures really mean, you need to look at the whole picture.'

'How do you do that?' she asked him.

'I like to observe somebody before they're in the interview situation, get a feel for their personality. Location can also have an impact, people are much more confident on their home territory. Then it's facial expressions, body language, the actual words they say, and how they say them. You have to add all of these together in order to get a full picture of what a person is saying subconsciously as well as consciously. It takes practice.'

'So, was there an answer where you were sure he was lying?'

Harrison thought for a moment. There'd been a few grey areas, and some blatant avoiding, but there was one answer which said a lot more than Sam had intended. 'When DI Painter asked Sam if the fight had been because Dax had found out something which Sam didn't want him to know, did you notice how Sam reacted?'

'He said "no comment", didn't he?'

'He did, but it was how he said it. There was a tiny nod of his head, which leaked a positive reply, plus a little shrug of one shoulder, and a look away from DI Painter. He also lowered the volume of his reply, and these tiny signs all told me he wasn't sure about how he was answering this. Afterwards, his body language also temporarily showed anxiety. So, you see, it wasn't one gesture, but a whole succession of them, which makes me think that if he was being honest, he'd have answered yes to that question, or at the very least he was unsure.'

Sally was focusing on his every word.

'Likewise, you can't say that a certain behaviour has just one specific meaning,' Harrison continued. 'Look at DI Painter. He's shifted his body to one side slightly, which someone could say indicates that he's not interested in what Sam is saying, or wants to distance himself from the discussion. However, I've noticed that he has a slight limp and winces sometimes when he gets up. That therefore leads me to the conclusion that he has a hip or lower back issue and the shift to one side is to take pressure off that sore hip and leg. His face looks engaged, so that adds to my conclusion.'

'Why did you decide to study psychology and learn all this?' Sally asked.

'Honestly? It was because I wasn't very good at connecting with people when I was younger. I know some people might say I'm not good at it now, but I wanted to understand the mind better so that I could understand people and their actions. The ritualistic elements were already an interest that had come from childhood experiences. Then I realised I could make a difference and get justice for victims.'

'I'm going to watch the video replay,' Sally said, her eyes shining with the possibility of a new-found skill.

For DI Painter and DS Reid, the interview had been a frustrating one, but Harrison had learnt something. There was very clearly something that Sam didn't want anyone knowing – but what was it? What had Dax discovered and why had it led to their argument?

27

Back in the incident room, DI Painter scrubbed at his eyes and forehead while he talked to Harrison after Sam's interview, and waited for whoever was in the station to gather for a briefing. He looked older, and considerably more tired than he had when Harrison had first met him two days ago; like a man who was ready to retire.

'Yes, I think I agree with you,' Painter was saying to Harrison. 'Much as I'm pained to admit it, I don't think Sam would have the patience and intelligence to plan a murder like Dax's. It's not his style. He'd just thrash it out there and then.'

'Doesn't mean he didn't kill Summer,' Harrison replied. 'That was more his style, and she was killed by somebody she knew.'

'You're still convinced we're looking at two different killers?'

'Yes. But I am interested in finding out what it was that Sam and Dax argued about because that could relate to his murder. It could also be related to what he found out at the library, which means Summer knew.'

'Agreed. I still think Chester is lying about their disagreement, and two arguments on the same day can't be a coincidence. We can't keep Sam in because there's just not enough evidence against him. I'm going to have to cut him loose. That counsel of his is itching to prove himself and I don't fancy being on the receiving end of a lawsuit for wrongful arrest. I want to enjoy the start of my retirement. I think we need to go and shake things up at the Holmes's household. Summer worked for them, so there's that link there, too.'

While they were talking, DS Reid had walked up with an armful of sandwiches, crisps, and fizzy drinks, which he put down on the desk in front of DI Painter.

'Here you go, boss, fill yer boots. Harrison, you sure you don't want anything? A big bloke like you ought to eat something.'

'I'm fine. Thank you,' Harrison replied politely.

'Maybe Dax had a go at Sam for suggesting he talk to Chester about expanding his business. If Chester did knock him back, maybe Dax felt humiliated and was annoyed at Sam for putting him in that position,' DS Reid said, adding to their conversation in between a mouthful of bacon crisps.

'Possible.' Painter nodded.

The two men sat down and focused on working their way through the pile of food.

Harrison left them to their eating and slipped off to check his phone for messages.

There was a new text message alert and Harrison's heart froze. Was it from them again? The anxiety that washed through his body made him angry. This had to stop.

The text was from Tanya. He clicked on it with relief flooding through his system. Then he read it.

Thanks for the beautiful roses. Love them x

She also sent a photograph of the bouquet on her kitchen worktop.

Harrison forgot to breathe for a few moments. He put out a hand to steady himself on one of the desks.

'Told you you'd get low blood sugar,' DS Reid shouted at him from behind, but Harrison barely heard him.

He'd not sent roses to Tanya.

He thought quickly and texted back. *I wasn't sure if they'd get the message right. What did they put on the card in the end?*

She sent a photograph back almost straight away.

To the rose in my life. With love forever, Harrison

You're going soft in your old age, she texted shortly after.

He didn't reply. Couldn't reply. He waited a few moments, then typed, *Sorry, something's just come up here. Speak soon.*

What could he say to her? She would be mortified that the roses weren't from him. It was only last year that she'd had all the trouble with the stalker sending her gifts. This was the last thing she needed. It was also the last thing he needed. They were clearly hammering home the message they'd sent yesterday, making it clear they weren't bluffing. His head was ringing. Fists balled. They were cowards hiding in the shadows. He would find them.

'Harrison, Dr Lane? We're starting the briefing now. Thought we'd better get on with it before you flake out.' DS Reid's voice broke through the haze of red mist that had descended. 'If you need a quick sugar hit, I've still got a spare flapjack,' he added jokingly.

Harrison had to pull himself together. He already knew that they had Tanya's address. This didn't change anything. As long as he didn't contact anyone else or wasn't seen to be investigating, then she'd be fine. He'd worry about what he was going to say to Tanya when he got to London.

'I went to interview Steven Bellowes,' DS Reid was saying to the assembled team. 'He's another member of the Ragnarok group that Summer, Dax, and Sam are part of. A solid alibi for both murders. The guy works as a train driver and was on shift for both. He said there was no obvious tension between any of them that he'd seen. They'd all known each other for a few years and saw each other socially, but not in each other's pockets, and he thought that Dax and Summer were probably the closest. He was surprised to hear that Dax may have had a fight. He reckoned that Dax was a gentle guy, and he'd never seen him angry. Couldn't think of anyone who would want to harm him. He did allude to some tensions in the group with Patrick wanting them to get more serious, as he put it, with their protests, and I got the feeling Patrick and Steven didn't always see eye to eye.'

'No Viking connections? Wasn't having a relationship with Summer?'

DS Reid shook his head at both questions. 'Not according to him.'

'Lovely bloke, that's what everyone says about Dax, but he had arguments with two men on the same day, one of which resulted in physical violence. There was something serious going on – at least in Dax's eyes,' DI Painter said.

'Looks that way.'

'How about any potential enemies from the environmental campaigning?'

'There was nothing on record for Dax, but we did get a hit with Patrick Sheldon. He was arrested a few months ago when a radical group of environmental protestors firebombed the offices of a development company. The business was seeking a planning application to tear down a copse of trees which are smack bang in the middle of their proposed site. Patrick was released without charge due to insufficient evidence. Two others are awaiting trial, and investigators believe there were at least three other individuals who were involved on that night.'

'Do we know anything about the developers? What kind of outfit are they? We took down that development company for laundering drugs money a couple of years ago. Get them checked out as you never know who might be behind the marketing facade and therefore what lengths they might go to in retaliation.'

'Will do, boss.'

'That also fits with what Sam said. Patrick wanting to take the group down a more radical route. Do we know where Dax was on the day this took place?'

'Not yet. He's not easy to keep tabs on because he never seemed to keep regular hours and spent a great deal of time in the forest, according to his phone records.'

'What else have we found from his phone records?' DI Painter looked over at a civilian analyst sitting towards the back.

'Nothing yet that indicates he was meeting anyone on the day of his murder, or was in any kind of trouble. It's all pretty innocuous stuff. A few client texts, part-time job applications, that's all, but we're digging deeper in case things have been deleted. Obviously we've only got limited data as we don't yet have the handset.'

'And Summer?'

'Phone is also missing, so we're having to go through the process of getting access to her records. It's turned off.'

'What about the gay community? Anyone made any headway there? It could be a lovers' tiff or someone who is homophobic.'

'We've been showing a photo of Dax around all the usual gay bars and clubs, and I've spoken to Matt Holloway, who runs Pride locally. Nobody has seen him or recognises him as being a part of their community,' DC Gorman said. 'Oh, and he laughed when I asked him if he knew any Vikings.'

'Bloody hell, another dead end there.'

'Sir, there's a new report come in that might be of interest.' DC Wellington spoke up now. 'A farmer has just reported that one of his sheep was killed and dismembered again, like a few weeks ago when it was blamed on the wolfman.'

'Where was this?'

'About half a mile from the car park for the woods.'

'Sir?' DC Sally Gorman raised a hand for DI Painter's attention. 'I've just been looking into that original sheep killing to check any links, and what's interesting is that a wooden spear was used to kill the sheep, just like the one that was used against Dax.'

'OK, Pete, check out the latest killing, would you?' he said, looking at the detective. 'This elusive wolfman is beginning to get on my proverbials. We need to have another go at tracking him down and flushing him out of those trees. He could be behind all this. And someone check to see if any violent prisoners from this area have been released lately, especially if they have a penchant for Vikings. I'm going to put in a request for helicopter and drone support as well as give the dogs another go. In the meantime, I want to go pay the Holmes family another visit. Summer worked for them, and I'm still not convinced about Chester's alibi for Dax, so let's go see if he's got a better one for early this morning.'

28

'There goes a vanload of sugar-laden dreams,' DS Reid said wistfully as DI Painter made way for a Bemford Cupcakes van on the driveway to the Holmes farm. 'Do you think we could seize some cupcakes as part of our inquiry?'

DI Painter smiled at his colleague's comments. 'Not sure we could arrest a cupcake for murder.'

Harrison was sitting in the back of the car again, silent, his thoughts on Tanya arranging a bouquet of red roses in a vase.

As they pulled up in front of the house, a silhouette peered out from one of the windows and within thirty seconds, Phillip Holmes was opening the front door.

'What is it this time, officers? Don't tell me you've come to harass my son again? I am going to have to call a solicitor.'

'Mr Holmes, I wonder if we might have a word?' DI Painter said to him. 'Is Chester at home?'

'What is this about? You're not still trying to pin that tree hugger's death on him, are you? I told you. He was here at home all evening.'

'No. It's not about Dax Moore.'

Phillip Holmes hesitated, as though his mind was running

through what the agenda would be this time, and he was trying to decide whether to play along or obstruct.

'Well, he's not here. He was at a party last night and stayed over,' he said triumphantly.

'I see. Would it be possible to have a word with you and your wife then instead? And if you could let us know where Chester is, then we'd appreciate it.'

'Are you going to tell me what this is about?' he asked them.

'Can you get your wife and we'll fill you both in,' DI Painter patiently replied.

'She's down with the horses. Our groom rang in sick and so she's having to deal with them.'

'I'll go and find her,' Harrison volunteered and started walking off towards the stables before anyone could argue otherwise.

Harrison was glad the opportunity had arisen. For one thing, he wanted to get Dawn Holmes on her own, away from her husband, and he also wanted to see where Summer worked. Behind him, he could hear DI Painter asking Phillip when it was that Summer had phoned in sick. Phillip seemed more concerned about what Harrison was doing rather than answering.

Harrison walked fast, keen to make the most of the time, just in case Phillip Holmes decided to take back control.

The stables were a fairly new wooden build, which looked out over the paddock. There were six stalls, and a tack and feed room. Harrison couldn't see Dawn immediately, but the sound of a woman's voice talking led him down to the end of the stalls.

'Mrs Holmes?' he called out, not wanting to startle her by suddenly appearing at the door.

'Who is it?'

'Dr Harrison Lane. I was here the other day with the police.'

He came up alongside the box and peered into the gloom. Dawn had a muck fork in her hand, the large, widespread prongs of the tool holding a small pile of manure which she deposited into a bucket.

'What is it now?' she asked.

'We wondered if you'd join your husband up at the house,' Harrison said.

'Why? Has something happened to Chester?' Her eyes opened in fear as every mother's worst nightmare flickered through her mind.

'No. It's not Chester. As far as I know, he is absolutely fine.'

Harrison saw her let out the breath she'd been holding on to. He tried to normalise their conversation to put her at ease.

'Do you ride as well, Mrs Holmes?'

'I do. I try to go out most days.'

'But this is one of the polo ponies, isn't it?'

'Yes. He's lame at the moment. I think Chester was sold a bit of a dud, if I'm honest. He's had problems with his legs ever since he got him.'

'I bet that keeps the vet in business,' Harrison replied, keen to put her at ease.

'Well, he just gives him what he can. Summer's been making up a poultice that she puts on his leg. That seems to work.'

'Did she not put one on yesterday?' Harrison asked, looking at the horse, which was clearly avoiding putting weight on one of its back legs.

'Yes, but Phillip doesn't like her doing it, so he took it off last evening. He reckons she's not qualified.'

'And what do you think, Mrs Holmes?' Harrison watched her as she stared at the horse.

Dawn Holmes thought a moment then turned round and looked at him defiantly. 'Summer said she's some kind of a witch and Phillip comes from a strict Catholic upbringing, so naturally he's wary.' She had reverted to dedicated wife mode. 'I'll just put these away and be right with you,' she added as she came out of the stall carrying the bucket and muck fork.

'What does Chester think about Summer's magic?' Harrison asked.

'I think he finds her interesting. Pretty girl with her pagan ways.'

'Have they been having a relationship then?'

'No, absolutely not. His father wouldn't approve for one thing and she's just a groom.'

Harrison didn't like the tone in her voice.

'He's out now?'

'Yes. With a friend from polo. House party in London. No doubt a wild one, as they all stayed over. Phillip was up very early to get things opened up at the factory.'

The pair of them had started to walk back towards the house.

'Has Summer ever read the runes for you?' Harrison asked.

'Absolutely not. I don't believe in that kind of rubbish.'

'Do you get involved in the business much?' Harrison was looking at the big industrial cupcake warehouse right in front of them.

'No. Not really. I'm also gluten intolerant so I don't eat the damned things. They do smell good but you get immune to it after a while.'

'So you don't know how many people work there?'

Dawn shook her head.

'Not that many. It's very automated.'

Harrison made a mental note to speak to DI Painter about getting the full staff list off Phillip in case the killer was working under their noses.

'I'll just go and wash my hands and take my boots off. Be right with you,' Dawn said to him.

Harrison joined Painter and Reid in the Holmes's sitting room, where a tense discussion was underway about what had happened to the farming side of the family business. Harrison slipped in and waited for Dawn to join them.

'We're not allowed to put this and that on the land, and what we can use has rocketed in price. They just don't care about the producers. All that matters is that the supermarkets can sell things as cheaply as possible.'

Dawn walked into the room and DI Painter wasted no time in using her arrival to get down to business and off the farming topic.

'I'm very sorry to have to inform you that this morning we found the body of Summer Frances. We believe she had been murdered.'

Dawn let out a gasp, her hand shooting to her mouth. 'Oh my God,' she said, and looked at her husband, who let out an exaggerated sigh.

'Was it something to do with Dax's death?' Phillip asked Painter.

'We suspect that the two murders are connected,' the detective replied. 'When did you last see Ms Frances?'

'She was here yesterday morning,' Dawn replied.

'And was she acting normally?'

'Well, no,' Dawn said, looking again at her husband. 'She'd just heard about Dax, so was very upset.'

'Of course,' Painter replied. 'But apart from the grief for her friend, was she scared or worried about anything?'

'I'm not sure she'd tell me,' Dawn replied.

'How well did you know Ms Frances?'

'We knew of her. She was our groom, but I can't say we ever really spoke to her much,' Phillip cut in before his wife could answer.

'But Chester was quite close to her?' Painter pushed.

'Close?' Phillip's eyes narrowed.

'Yes. Weren't they friendly?' Painter replied.

'He was her boss. They rode out together several days a week, if that's what you mean.'

Harrison wondered if Phillip Holmes realised that he was coming across as being completely compassionless.

'And you say that Summer rang you late yesterday and said she wouldn't be in today?'

'That's correct,' Phillip replied. 'I'm sure you'll see the call on the phone records.'

DI Painter paused a moment.

'Could you let us know where you were first thing this morning, Mr Holmes?' Harrison asked.

'I was at home here with my wife. We both got up at around eight and had breakfast together. Porridge and coffee if you want to know. Then I took a shower and went across to the factory about nine.' Phillip's face was rigid, his muscles tensed and jaw tight. 'I do hope I'm not going to need a lawyer, too, detective?'

'I'm not a detective, Mr Holmes. I'm a psychologist,' Harrison replied. He wasn't usually so curt with people, but something about Phillip Holmes rubbed him up the wrong way.

Phillip clearly didn't know how to respond.

DI Painter filled the silence.

'So Chester was at a party last night, you say?' he asked, taking out his notebook.

'Yes. Friend of his who he plays polo with.'

'Does this friend have a name?'

'Well, of course he does, detective. Sorry, I am presuming *you're* a detective,' Phillip said to DI Painter sarcastically. 'Angus Forester-Jones. He's got a place in Battersea, London. If you're looking for witnesses I think you'll find there were plenty of highly respected young men there. I believe a Viscount and a Lord were on the guest list.'

'OK. Thank you, both of you, for your time,' Painter replied without showing any signs that he'd been impressed by the name dropping. 'Once again, apologies for having to be the bearer of bad news.' DI Painter stood up and Freddie and Harrison followed him out.

Once in the car, Painter turned to Harrison. 'What made you ask Phillip where he was this morning?'

'His complete lack of surprise or compassion when you told him Summer was dead, and the fact his wife told me that he was up very early this morning and went straight across to the factory, but he maintains he rose at eight and had breakfast with her.'

'You think Phillip might be our killer? Why? What's his motive?'

'I'm certainly suspicious, let's put it that way. He wasn't a fan of Summer, according to Mrs Holmes. As for motive, I don't know yet.'

'Bloody hell. I can't see him sleeping with Summer, but then maybe I'm being blind. Perhaps she liked older men with money.'

Ideas were forming and morphing in Harrison's head, but nothing made any sense without motive. To make headway on that, he felt sure he needed to follow the trail to the library.

29

By the time they returned to the incident room, it was too late for Harrison to get to the library. He decided to go first thing in the morning and checked what time it opened. It had been a busy day, and the emotion brought on by the latest text from Tanya was draining him.

Harrison didn't need to worry about dinner because he was fasting, but he began to wonder if the lack of food was also making him more tired. Some days the fasting made his brain work better, helped him to feel more energised and awake. The old Neolithic bodily instinct that he was hungry and therefore needed to have his wits about him so he could go and hunt himself the next meal. Occasionally, it made him feel slightly muddle-headed, unable to concentrate, and tired. Today, he felt as if all the energy had been bled from his muscles.

He could try to blame his slow mental and physical state on the lack of blood sugar, but if he was honest, it was more likely emotional exhaustion coupled with the busy day at work. His intention, therefore, was to head to bed for an early night, and rest. Wake up tomorrow morning, eat a hearty breakfast and head to the library.

Before he went to sleep, Harrison checked in with his assistant, Ryan.

'Yo, boss. Are you back home now?'

'No. We had another murder.'

'More from the Viking?'

'Supposedly, but I think we have two killers on the go now. I need to stay here for at least another day. I don't want another corpse.'

'Fair enough.'

'Everything alright with work?'

'Yeah, all quiet, just the usual,' Ryan replied.

'New flat working out OK still?'

'Yeah, love it. Nice small windows.'

That made Harrison smile and an image appeared in his head of Ryan, moving around Harrison's flat during his stay like a beach limpet, from one piece of furniture to another while all the time avoiding the huge windows that overlooked the Thames in his Dockland apartment.

'I guess my place isn't ideal when you have agoraphobia,' he replied.

'I was certainly grateful for the safe house when I needed it,' Ryan said, and Harrison knew he was genuinely grateful. Ryan's past had caught up with him just before Christmas and they'd had to undertake an emergency evacuation of Ryan's old flat. Staying with Harrison had been the safest option.

'So what are you doing tonight?' Harrison asked, changing the emotional subject.

'Just about finished emptying all the boxes and found my replica Lord of the Rings Horn of Gondor today. Haven't watched the films in a while so I'm going to binge watch the whole Tolkien trilogy courtesy of Peter Jackson tonight.'

Harrison understood about half of what Ryan had just said, but enough to get the gist that he was going to be watching film adaptations of the books.

'Enjoy. Speak soon,' Harrison had simply replied. He heard the giggle in Ryan's voice as he returned the goodbye. Ryan would know that Harrison had never watched the films.

Harrison sighed as he ended the phone call. It had been good to speak to Ryan. He had reminded him of his flat and office – the places he felt secure. Home.

Outside, he could hear people moving about the corridor, chatting and laughing. A child's footsteps running. A door slamming. A raised voice. Music. Life was going on around him, oblivious. It made him feel alone. While he had always sought solitude in the past, Tanya had opened his soul to this alien feeling. Her presence was like an earworm song that you couldn't forget and hummed subconsciously. Always there.

He tried to analyse himself. It was as though he had started to suffer from a kind of bereavement. The loss of someone loved, the sadness of a shared life no more. Harrison realised that subconsciously, he had made the decision to end their relationship. He had to protect her. He knew it was the right thing to do. But it would come at a price – one he now rationalised. They were just feelings after all, not cold hard facts. The pain wasn't physical. He would get over it with time.

Harrison put his earbuds in and chose Lewis Capaldi from his playlist. He needed more than acoustic music to carry his mind away. He listened to every word of 'Pointless'. As he finally fell into a deep sleep, a single tear escaped from the corner of his eye onto the hotel pillow, betraying the turmoil inside his mind.

30

He waited for the woman to go to bed. He'd stayed crouched in some bushes in her back garden, watching. The slight drizzle of rain didn't bother him, but the cold seeped through into his bones. He'd chosen this house because he knew they didn't have a dog. No early warning alarm to tell the woman that he was there.

He didn't want to do it. This was not who he was. Who he wanted to be again. It was just a temporary state of desperation. That's what he kept telling himself. A part of him wanted to just give up, but it was fear that kept him going. Fear that he'd end up back there. It meant he had to keep moving forward; standing still or going back was not an option.

He waited until the lights had gone out in the whole house and then he'd crept out from under the bush and flitted across the garden through the moonlight. The green wheelie bin was tall and heavy so he couldn't tip it. Instead, he grabbed at the top bin bag and pulled it down onto the ground, hunger growling in his belly.

There was something hard inside and it clonked against the concrete path. It sounded loud in the still of the night, but not as loud as the dog next door which had heard it. The beast began to bark, shouting a warning to its household. The woman's lights stayed off. He froze like a rabbit. His hesitation was his undoing.

Lights flooded the back garden of the neighbouring house and he heard a man's voice.

'What is it, Hugo?'

The fence was low enough for the man to look over. He saw him walk into his own garden and search, but the dog wasn't fooled. It launched itself at the fence between the gardens, barking madly. It would be just seconds before the man looked over and saw him. He ran.

'Hey, hey! Stop! I'm calling the police,' he heard the man shouting.

He vaulted the fence at the end of the garden and ran back towards safety.

The dark mass of the forest was in front of him. He careered through the streets full of houses where people lived their neat lives; law abiding members of their communities, born into a world that understood them. He ran, heart pounding, breath burning in and out of his lungs, through the field and into the trees. Back to where he couldn't be seen. Where he could meld into the shadows and disappear.

31

Harrison woke up to a grey morning which perfectly matched his mood. His dreams had been filled with disturbing imagery. Summer's dead eyes and Tanya scared and in danger. For a few moments he'd lain on the bed feeling heavy, as though a weight was bearing down on his chest. He understood this feeling. The desire to just stay locked away in this room, lying in the curtained shade of day and refusing to face the world. It was a feeling he'd had before, a long time ago when he had just become a man and his mother had been lost to him. The image of Dax, a young man with his life ahead of him, hanging, life spent, came into his mind. He heaved himself from the bed and went into the shower.

There wasn't a hunger in his stomach when he went down for breakfast. Quite often after fasting, he'd pass the initial urge for food and it wouldn't strike again until later, but today it was muted further by his mood. He knew he had to eat because he wanted to be on top form and when working like this, he could never be sure where the next meal was coming from. Harrison piled his plate with pastries and ordered a full English breakfast. His first port of call was going to be the library.

. . .

The library was a fifteen-minute drive from the hotel and Harrison was at the doors five minutes before they were unlocked. It was an old building, but the service had been modernised with machines to self-check books in and out and just one desk visible with a human being to talk to.

The librarian was a woman in her forties with a long bob style haircut that she'd dyed a violet colour. Her jumper proudly declared *I Would Rather be Reading*. She was tapping away on her computer as Harrison strode up to her. In fact, she was concentrating so hard on what she was writing that when she looked up to see him, she was almost startled.

'How can I help?' she asked once she'd recovered her composure.

Harrison took out his ID. 'I understand that Dax Moore was a regular visitor here?' he questioned, not entirely sure if the library had been a smoke screen, and he hadn't actually been a regular.

'Yes. Absolutely tragic what happened. Saw it in the paper. He was a lovely young man,' she said. 'Used to come in here a few times a week. Was hoping to go back to college. Such a shame.'

'Did he always sit in the same place?'

'Usually, yes. He would sit on the desks over there. Between you and me, I think part of the reason he came in so often was because he wanted to charge his mobile phone. Told me he lived in a caravan without any electricity. He could also get a hot drink here and read the papers. He liked to keep up with the news.'

Harrison looked over to where she was pointing.

'Was he reading or researching anything specific, do you know? Especially in the last week or so? I'm particularly thinking about last Friday. Did you see him in here, then?'

'Oh yes. He had asked for one of the reference books. Was

looking at the forest and local maps, you see. Had some idea about how he could develop his business, he told me.'

'Can you show me the book that he asked for?'

'Of course. You know, you're not the first one in here asking about Dax and what he'd been reading. A young lady came in day before yesterday. Said she was a friend of his and he'd asked her to finish off the project he'd been working on. She told me she wanted to do it for him. Seemed quite upset.'

'She wasn't a library member though, was she? So, did you register her?'

The librarian looked surprised. 'Well, no, she wasn't and yes, I did. It's free, anyone can join, you know. As long as they have ID.'

'Did you show her the same book that you're about to show me?'

'Yes. She stayed for half an hour or so and then left. I think it had upset her again. She looked like she was crying when she walked out. This is it.'

She pulled an innocuous paperback book from the shelf. It had the look of an amateur publisher, not a professional mass market kind of paperback. A local guidebook of sorts.

'Published in the early seventies. Surprised we still have a copy, to be honest. Nobody ever asks for it. At least not until Dax did.'

Harrison took the book and flicked through. It was a series of local landmarks with hand-drawn maps and walks plotted out.

'How did Dax seem when he read it?'

'Couldn't tell you, I'm afraid. I'd gone on my break and when I came back he'd gone.'

'And you're sure this is the only book that Dax and the young woman who came in looked at?'

'It's the only one they both looked at, yes. She just sat down and read through this one. Dax had a few others that he'd borrowed.'

'I'm going to have to borrow this,' Harrison said.

'You're not allowed to take that one out of the library, I'm afraid. It's reference only.'

'I'm sorry, I'm going to have to insist because I think this contains some vital evidence which will help the police inquiry to track down Dax's killer.'

Harrison had hold of the book firmly and wasn't about to let go of it. For a few seconds they faced each other off, but even his towering muscular form was no match for her iron will, bolstered by the rules. In the end, it was her compassion for Dax that won through.

'You really think it will find his killer?'

'I think it will help. Yes.'

'OK. I'll get a special permission form. Come back to the desk with me. You'll have to sign it out.' She started to walk back to her desk, and then stopped and turned, looking up at Harrison. 'I hope you get him and send him away for life.'

32

Harrison arrived at the incident room just as DI Painter was also pulling up in his car.

'Been to see Summer's parents,' the detective explained to him. 'They'd been away in Scotland and have just come back. They'd been informed of their daughter's death, but obviously had a lot of questions.'

DI Painter plodded into the incident room with sagging shoulders. Harrison certainly didn't envy him that job. It was usually one of the most disliked parts of any case like this. You knew you were talking to a family who had just had their world destroyed and would never be the same again. The raw grief that officers like DI Painter had to experience couldn't fail to leave a mark on their souls.

'I have the library book which both Dax and Summer looked at the day before they were killed,' Harrison said, showing him the innocuous title.

'You serious? You think that's somehow led to two murders?'

'Somehow, I think it is connected, yes.'

Painter puffed his chest, adjusted his shoulders, and sniffed. 'Well, if you find anything, let me know. We're tracking the movements of Sam Green, Patrick Sheldon, and Chester Holmes. I don't think any of them have been totally honest with us and I want to know why. I've also requested every available resource we have to search the woods for wolfman. There was another sighting of him last night. Apparently, he was in someone's back garden, not far from the woods. That's the first time we've had a report of him venturing out of the forest; if he is our murderer then maybe he's widened his hunting ground as the walkers are staying away. Management have agreed we can have access to the helicopter and I've got a dog team and a drone operator. The plan is to do a drone heat search and see if we can spot him, then send everyone in to round him up. We're rendezvousing at the woods for midday if you want to join us. Tactical are going to take the lead and run the search.'

'I'll be there,' Harrison replied. That gave him a good hour to look through the book and see if he could find what it was that had set off this chain of events.

Harrison found himself a quiet corner of the staff canteen and sat down with a chamomile tea and the book. He didn't know the area well and while he often believed that coming fresh to a crime scene without any prior knowledge was an advantage, in this instance, he wondered if perhaps it might be a disadvantage. He'd soon find out.

The first thing Harrison did was check out the author, a Terrence G. Plumber. He was an elderly man who was a keen hiker and had worked for the local authority all his career. When Harrison looked up his current whereabouts, he discovered that he'd died almost twenty years ago. Not surprising, he considered, seeing as he'd been in his early seventies in the 1970s. There was no obvious reason why he should be significant to their case.

The book turned out to be a series of circular walks around the district, all with a paragraph about objects or areas of interest, combined with local history. Every walk had its own hand-drawn map with the interesting things clearly labelled in a uniquely vintage seventies way.

Harrison spotted the Viking stone that Sally had mentioned on his first day here, but could find no other mention of any Viking objects or even history. He did, however, find a walk that encompassed the yew tree. Mr Plumber clearly appreciated the age and beauty of the tree, but wasn't interested in any spiritual or mythological stories around it. Harrison could see nothing in his description which was unusual or could warrant someone being murdered.

The clock on the canteen wall caught his eye and he realised he was going to have to head to the incident room and join the others in the search for wolfman. The book would have to wait for now.

DI Painter had a large paper map spread out over a table and the team were all standing around looking and pointing. Someone had marked the map with a pink highlighter pen. Painter was briefing the team.

'All the sightings we have, which are marked, are all in this area of the woods. Now that's not to say that he's definitely around here because this also happens to be the part where the public is allowed, so it's just possible he goes further in, but there are no witnesses. The sheep killings were here and here, Dax's caravan is here, and last night's sighting is here.'

Painter looked up at the faces, all concentrating on the geography in front of them. 'We are going to start with thermal imaging drones. We've got two and we're going to get them up and scanning the whole forest area. If we detect somebody, then I want the on-the-ground teams to move in, backed up by the dog unit. We've got two dog teams with us today as well. If we do require helicopter support, then it's available to us, but obviously I'm not going to run up our departmental bill unless it's really needed. To make this work, we're going to have to station several units around the woods so that you can get to whichever area we need you to be in quickly.'

'How do we know it's not just going to be a walker?' a uniformed officer asked.

'We can't know for sure, but we've had the car park closed off and a sign up warning the public not to enter the woods since early this morning. You've all seen the photofit of him. The guy's been living rough out in the woods, so I'm guessing his appearance is going to be a bit wild. He may well be suffering from a mental illness, so go easy for his safety and yours.'

'Are there any shelters in the woods? Anywhere he's likely to have been staying? I mean, the weather's been pretty crap lately, so how's he been living and sleeping?'

'That is a mystery I'm hoping we will solve today. The Forestry Commission has assured us that there are no buildings or structures in the woods. I'd have thought a tent is pretty risky as it could be spotted, unless he's either camouflaged it somehow, or just puts it up at night.'

'We dealing with some bloody Rambo character?' another officer asked.

'Let's hope not. I think we've got enough bodies on the ground and eyes in the sky to get him and bring him in.'

'Are we sure he's connected to the murders?' the same officer asked.

'We know he was spotted or had been near to both murder victims after death. Now that obviously doesn't mean he killed them, but he could at least be a material witness. I don't know what part, if any, he has played, but I do know I want this man found so we can at least eliminate him from our enquiries and ensure he's not a public risk. We'll have every available member of personnel in those woods. So let's make sure we get him this time.'

33

Harrison decided he'd get a better overview of the operation by sticking with DI Painter, who had teamed up with the tactical squad commander at the operational HQ in the forest car park. Here, the drone operators were relaying back the images, and Painter had full comms with all the teams in the woods.

The gravel car park was once again filled with emergency personnel vehicles instead of the colourful diversity of public cars. Where usually there would be excitable dogs of all sizes and varieties, setting off on their much anticipated walks, or returning tongues lolling, there were two dog team vans with their highly trained German shepherds. Two minibuses were parked partially blocking the entrance to ensure no public access during the operation. They'd delivered the teams of uniformed officers who were just getting into position across the woods. The rest of the detectives, tactical squad commander, and drone operator cars were scattered around the car park. Facing all of them was the dark green and brown forest, still holding on tight to its secrets.

While they waited for everyone to walk to their designated

holding positions in the woods, Painter paced around the car park nervously.

'I don't want any more deaths on my watch,' he said to Harrison. 'Do you think this man could be psychotic and think he's a Viking?'

'It doesn't fit. Dax was definitely killed by someone on horseback, and Summer was killed by a man in smart shoes, who likely drove a four-by-four car.'

'So you think I'm wasting time and resources with this?'

'No. Like you said, this man has been seen too many times to be a phantom and so he could be key to telling us what happened to Dax and Summer. If he creeps around the woods, it stands to reason that he might have seen or heard something. Either way, we have to be able to discount him. Question is, will his mental state be stable enough to be able to answer questions and help our inquiry?'

Painter sighed in agreement. 'I guess at the very least we could charge him with sheep rustling.'

'Sir, they're all in position and ready to start.' DC Gorman walked up to where Harrison and Painter were talking.

'Right. Let's get to it,' he replied with another deep sigh that Harrison could tell was full of nothing but hope.

'We've got one drone team here, and the other over there.' The tactical commander showed them. 'Both drones are now airborne and will do a systematic sweep. We know exactly where our men are and if we spot anyone, we'll get the nearest team to move in and intercept.'

The detectives, Harrison and the tactical commander were huddled around a series of small screens that variously showed the images from the drones, and the body cams worn by each of the team leaders. It was amazing how similar the body cam images were, row upon row of brown tree trunks, interspersed with the occasional flash of a high-vis jacket.

'If he's in there, we'll find him,' the commander said to them.

Nobody said a word for the next ten minutes as the drones scanned the forest below them for any signs of warm bodies. They watched as they flew over the various police teams, and hearts jumped with anticipation when an unknown heat source appeared. It quickly led to sighs as the outline of a deer became visible. Harrison could see DI Painter willing the drones to find something, but there was nothing except tree after tree after tree.

'We'll go over again,' the commander said to the audience of disappointed faces around him.

'Perhaps he got spooked and moved on,' DS Reid thought out loud. 'Wouldn't be surprising with all the police presence and our attempt to track him down with the dogs.'

'Maybe,' DI Painter reluctantly agreed.

The drones started their slow flight over the forest again. One concentrated on the eastern edge of the woods which backed onto the Holmes's land, and the other on the western flank. For a further ten minutes, they systematically covered the forest below them. Searching.

'Bloody hell,' DI Painter exclaimed as the drones, yet again, finished their missions. He muttered under his breath and stepped away from the screen, agitated.

'We've got enough battery for one more pass over,' the tactical commander said to him. 'I can't see that he's there, but as we are all here, we might as well do it.'

'Go for it. Got nothing to lose,' Painter sniffed.

The message was relayed to the drone operative on the eastern side of the forest, and the two machines started to fly back to their start positions.

'What's that?' DI Painter suddenly jabbed at the screen.

'That wasn't there a few seconds ago,' a disembodied voice

came over the radio from the drone operator. 'Looks to me like a human heat source. It could be a walker, but they've appeared out of nowhere.'

All of them craned to look at the moving orange figure on the grey screen.

'Beta unit, we have a figure moving north of you from the east. About two hundred yards away.'

'Copy. On the move.'

'He's heading in the direction of the yew tree clearing,' Harrison said.

'Alpha unit, engage as backup.' The commander was getting his teams into place. The figure seemed to be oblivious to the drone and was still heading in the same straight line. From the screen they could see the police team moving in behind, with the dog in the lead, heading straight for the figure, while another approached from the west side.

The figure suddenly stopped and looked around.

'He must be able to see or hear the dog by now,' Painter said.

'He's trying to work out which direction to run in,' Harrison added.

Behind the man, they could see the Beta unit closing in. Going back was now not an option for him. He started to run, heading for the yew tree clearing. To his side, Alpha unit was also getting closer.

'We've got visual,' the Beta unit lead said breathlessly through the radio microphone. 'Black-haired male with a beard.'

On the screen, Harrison and the rest of the team watched as the police dog closed in on the fleeing figure. He was at the clearing now and by the time he got across to the other side, the dog would be on him. Only he didn't cross to the other side. He stopped and started to climb the yew tree.

'What's he doing?' DI Painter said.

'Climbing the tree to get away from the dog,' the commander replied.

'We've got him.' DI Painter punched at the air. 'He's a sitting duck now.'

The juddery video from the Beta unit's body cam slowed down with the officer's pace, and the scene in the yew clearing came into view. The dog, a large Alsatian, was at the bottom of the tree, barking and jumping up at the main trunk. As the officers approached the tree, a figure could be seen clinging onto one of the thick branches.

'Police,' they shouted. 'Come down from the tree now and lie on the ground.'

The man's frightened face peered down at them.

'You're not under arrest. We just want to talk to you. We'll leash the dog,' the Beta team lead said to the man, and the dog was duly put back on his lead and led away from the tree for his reward.

'We have officers surrounding you. I don't want to have to send someone up to get you, but I will if you don't come down immediately. We just want to talk.'

The Alpha team arrived in the clearing and the two team leads had a discussion about how best to ensure the area was covered by officers and what to do to get the man down if he didn't come down voluntarily.

The wolfman seemed to have hidden further in the tree, trying to make himself invisible.

'I can still see you're up there,' the officer said to him. 'We are not going to hurt you. Please come down before anyone gets injured. What's your name?'

There was no reply and no indication that the man was going to move out of the tree.

Back in the car park, Harrison was getting concerned. 'I'm going to go in there and see if I can talk him down. If he's mentally ill, then the strong-arm tactic won't work.'

DI Painter and the tactical commander looked at each other.

'You're right,' Painter said. 'You're best placed to know how to deal with him. He seems to think we can't see him if he hides in the branches. That's not exactly rock solid sane if you ask me.'

Harrison didn't need any further encouragement. He was striding off across the car park and into the trees.

'Tell them to ease off until I get there,' he shouted back to them.

Behind him, he heard the tactical command officer relaying the situation to the teams.

'Dr Harrison Lane is heading to the clearing to assist with negotiations with our suspect. He's a psychologist. Step back from the tree and give the suspect some space, but don't take your eyes off him.'

Harrison broke into a fast jog. He had a fair distance to cover, but he was used to it, usually running about six miles most days at home. The path was relatively even, but he kept a close eye on where he was stepping, avoiding any tree roots and fallen branches, keeping a steady pace. The last thing he wanted was an injury; then he'd be no good to anyone. He needed to hurry up because if the man was mentally ill, the stressful situation would be making him worse.

When Harrison reached the clearing, the scene of what he'd been watching on the monitors lay before him in full colour. Police officers stood circling the tree, around ten feet away, with two dog units across the other side of the clearing, ready to act if needed but far enough away to diffuse the threat. They'd backed away, but for whoever was up the tree, it would still be an extremely stressful position to be in.

'Dr Lane?' The officer in charge of Beta unit met him as he walked into the clearing. Harrison recognised his voice from the audio feed they'd been listening to. 'He's still up the tree, hiding among the branches. He's difficult to see – tucked himself right into the trunk – but he fits the description of the wolfman.'

Harrison tipped his head to show he'd understood and slowly walked forward.

The officer was right. The wolfman had lodged himself right up against the tree trunk, about ten feet off the ground. Yews weren't particularly tall trees, which was advantageous as he might well have climbed a lot higher had it been a pine. The photographs of Dax were still pinned to the trunk of the tree, some showing rain damage, poignant reminders of what had happened here just a few days previously.

'Hi, my name is Dr Harrison Lane. I'm here to help you. The police officers don't want to hurt you, they just want to talk to you. Would you tell me your name?'

He waited, but there was no reply.

'I can ask for the dogs to be taken away if they're bothering you.'

Still nothing.

'This is a very special tree. Do you like this tree?'

Nothing.

'You've been living in the forest, haven't you? I expect it's been cold and wet over the winter. You must be tired. I can get you a nice warm bed and a good meal if you come with me?'

Harrison craned to see the man's face. He was still hidden behind the branches of green yew needles. Without visual contact, it was incredibly difficult to gauge what state the man's mental health was in and if he was taking in anything that Harrison was saying to him.

'Will you come down from the tree, please?' Harrison tried again, softly.

The branches rustled, and the face of a man appeared. He had shoulder-length black hair and a beard, as had been described by the various witnesses, but he didn't look like Harrison had expected. His face was clean and the beard neatly trimmed. He looked Middle Eastern in origin and that made Harrison wonder if perhaps one of the reasons he wasn't replying was because he didn't understand English.

'Hello,' Harrison said again to him, smiling. 'You must have been very frightened by the dog and police officers chasing you. You're not under arrest, we would just like to talk.'

The man stared at him. Harrison could tell he was weighing him up, trying to judge if he could be trusted in any way.

'Are you ready to come down?' Harrison asked again, this time acting out the action of jumping down from the tree.

The man's face was pale and his eyes scanned the police officers in the clearing before coming back to rest on Harrison. Then, slowly, he began to move, shuffling his feet and edging his body along the branch.

'Careful.' Harrison put his hands out for him to stop.

The man stayed focusing on him, eyes locked on his. He put both his hands on the branch and swung his body weight down towards the ground, dropping the last few feet like a cat. He was slightly built, athletic, wearing jogging bottoms and a warm fleece. His clothes weren't totally clean, but again, they weren't the well-used rags that Harrison would have expected for someone living out in the woods for weeks on end.

The Beta team officer stepped forward, and the man flinched away.

Harrison put his hand up to the officer. 'Hand me the cuffs,' he said to him.

The officer walked over to him and gave him the handcuffs. 'Watch him. He could have a knife.'

Harrison turned back to the man and smiled. 'Do you want to tell me your name?'

The man seemed to think for a moment and then replied, 'Hassan.'

Harrison smiled at him again. 'Would you sit on the floor for me, Hassan? I'm going to have to put these on you, but just until we get out of the woods. They're as much for your safety as for ours. Then we're going to go for a walk and a drive and I'll get you that meal I promised you.'

Hassan shook his head. 'I'm not going back,' he said. His accent was strong, but his English was good.

'Have you been in a detention centre?' Harrison asked him.

Hassan nodded. 'Refused asylum. If you send me back, they will torture me. I'm not going back.'

'We can get you legal representation to fight deportation,' Harrison replied. 'You can appeal.'

Hassan shook his head as though he thought it useless.

Harrison noticed that since he'd come down from the tree, a fresh sweat had broken out on Hassan's forehead. His skin looked pale and clammy. Had he taken some drugs, or was it a stress reaction?

Hassan sat down heavily on the forest floor.

Harrison walked slowly towards him and dropped down to a crouch beside him, never losing eye contact.

'Were you friends with Dax?' he asked.

Hassan's face changed completely. A wave of grief washed over his features and his eyes dropped to the floor. He didn't need to answer.

'Did you kill Dax?'

'No,' Hassan looked back up at Harrison, fire back in his eyes.

'I believe you, but we need to find out who did kill Dax. That's why we need you to help us. You've seen things, haven't you?'

'Don't know,' Hassan only barely whispered. 'He was gone.'

'What about Summer?' Harrison coaxed. 'I know you saw her body.'

Hassan hung his head. Grief seemed to have weighted his slim frame, sucking all energy from him.

'OK. I'm going to put these on now and we'll get you somewhere warm and comfortable,' Harrison said, indicating the handcuffs which he slipped over Hassan's thin wrists. Then he turned to the Beta team leader and signalled that they were ready to start moving.

Two police officers came forward and took one arm each, lifting Hassan off the ground. As they did so, he doubled over and retched. Hassan suddenly looked wobbly. His legs didn't seem to want to support him. Was he bluffing? Was it the shock of being chased and caught? Or was something else wrong? He no longer looked like the agile, fit man who had jumped from the tree earlier.

'Have you taken something?' Harrison asked him.

Hassan looked as if he were about to collapse. His lips moved, but barely any sound came out. 'Not going back.'

Harrison just caught his words.

'His pupils are dilated. Search his pockets for drugs,' the Beta team leader said to one of the officers.

One of them quickly frisked Hassan down. He found nothing.

Hassan's legs buckled beneath him. He seemed to be drowsy and was only being held up by the officers on either side of him.

'Lie him down,' the Beta team leader barked to his officers and then into his radio, 'We're going to need medical support.'

Harrison stood aside as the trained police officers checked Hassan's vital signs.

'His heart rate's going crazy,' an officer said to the team leader. 'We need to get him out of here quickly before he goes into cardiac arrest.'

'OK, we've no idea what he's taken. Let's carry him between us and head for the car park as fast as we can. We can meet the paramedics there, it will be quicker.'

Harrison could hear the voices at the command centre in the car park, shouting for medical backup. All he could think about was what Hassan had said to him: 'I'm not going back.' Had he taken a fatal dose of something?

As the dogs and the two teams started to move out of the

clearing, Harrison was about to follow them when he had an idea. He searched for where Hassan had been sick. It was fairly easy to detect because on the forest floor all the leaves and needles were brown, fallen from their branches and rotting back into the earth to help produce new life. The yew needles that Hassan had vomited back were green.

'He's eaten yew needles,' Harrison shouted after them. 'They're highly poisonous. Tell the paramedics it's taxines from the yew, but they need to hurry. I think we might already be too late to save him.'

34
___

As the clearing emptied and the voices and radios of the police teams disappeared along the path, Harrison didn't move. He knew Hassan wouldn't make it. He'd looked into his eyes and seen the void where life and hope should have been. He'd also seen medical reports from other people who'd been poisoned by yew needles and berries, and there was very little that the nurses and doctors could do to stop the poison from ravaging a person's body and making their heart fail.

Harrison felt tired again. The adrenaline rush was over, and the emotional toll of the case and his own private life weighed heavily on him. He found a fallen tree and sat down. He needed quiet.

Without the noise and activity of humans, the forest regained its natural order. Birds returned to the trees around him, and he listened to their songs and calls as they busied themselves with life. Dax was right. Immersing yourself in the forest was good for the soul. He'd seen the surveys that said nine out of ten people had improved well-being after listening to birdsong. Just a few minutes of sitting and being surrounded by nature was already helping him to claw back from the edge of the deep pit of despair that threatened his mind.

Sometimes, he just needed to stop and to recharge. Everyone needed that. No one was a robot.

He thought it no wonder that Dax and Summer had found this clearing magical, sacred even. Undoubtedly, countless people before them would have felt the same way. It wasn't a particularly sunny day, but being in a pool of pale light with the mystical ancient yew tree was spiritual at its most basic level. The Norse people and Vikings were animists. They believed that all natural phenomena have a soul or spirit and that humans were just a part of the natural network. They understood the connection between mind and body.

Harrison contemplated Summer's words and thought how the Norse people's deep relationship with the trees and plants of the natural world around them was so much more holistic and wholesome than industrial age lifestyles where people interacted with plants and animals purely as consumers.

He closed his eyes and breathed in the forest air, feeling its cleansing touch as it was drawn into his lungs and then out again. His controlled breathing began to slow his brain. It had been like a dynamo, still spinning even when he'd tried to rest. So many things to think about. So much pressure.

When Harrison opened his eyes again, the yew was the first thing he saw. It stood there still and yet full of life. Never dying. Witness to Harrison, to Dax and Summer, to the thousands of people who had looked upon it over the generations. Its evergreen needles, which symbolised life and rebirth, were highly poisonous to humans, and yet paradoxically, the tree also contained cancer-fighting taxol, which could save people's lives. Nature was like that, healing and yet deadly.

Harrison thought about Hassan. He wasn't their killer, but he was connected to Dax. Was he Dax's mysterious lover? Did he not want to go back to a place where homosexuals were persecuted? He said he hadn't known who killed Dax. Was this another dead end for the investigation? He didn't think Hassan could be the information that Dax, Sam, and Chester argued about, so what was it? He needed to get back to the incident room and take another look at that book.

By the time Harrison reached the car park, a morbid silence had settled on its occupants. There was no sign of the ambulance or Hassan.

'Do you think he'll make it?' DC Gorman came up to greet Harrison.

He looked at her earnest face. 'I don't think so,' he replied.

'They ran all the way here with him and the paramedics did their best. He's on his way to the hospital now. There might be some hope.'

'Maybe,' Harrison said to her gently.

'What the hell happened in there?' DI Painter had walked over now. He looked like he was about to have a cardiac episode, too. His face was flushed and his whole body tense with anxiety.

'He's a refugee, refused asylum, must have escaped one of the detention centres. Said that he wasn't going back. He ate the yew tree needles which are highly poisonous. I suppose this was a better option for him than whatever awaited him at home.'

'Bloody hell. There's going to be an inquiry into this. Did he say anything else? Mention Dax or Summer?'

'I asked him if he was a friend of Dax's and he looked devastated when I mentioned his name.'

'So you think they were connected?'

'I think so,' Harrison replied. 'I wouldn't be surprised if he turned out to be Dax's partner.'

'Right. Did you get a name?'

'Just Hassan.'

'OK. Freddie, get onto it, would you? Get a photograph of

Hassan from the body cam footage and send it to the immigration authorities. Let's find out where he's from and how he's involved in this mess.'

Two hours later, the flat mood at the car park had turned into one of resigned depression in the incident room. The officer who had accompanied Hassan to the hospital had rung in to say he was dead on arrival. The paramedics had been unable to save him.

DI Painter had been gone for nearly an hour explaining the day's events and their lack of progress in the inquiry to his bosses on the management floor. Harrison had been sitting nursing a hot cup of chamomile tea for so long that it was now cold. He felt tired, wrung out, and he was trying to clear his mind, trying to see how all the pieces fitted together.

DI Painter came back into the incident room in fighting mood, despite the odds stacking against them. 'We have three dead bodies and absolutely no idea why two of them were murdered. All of you quit the long faces and let's go through everything we know about the victims again. There has to be a clue or a motive somewhere.'

The room shifted like seaweed on the tide, moving towards the front of the room and the screen, which currently showed an immigration centre ID photograph of Hassan. The mixed bag of detectives, uniformed officers and civilian staff settled into their seats and waited for DI Painter to start.

'So, we now know that the wolfman was Hassan Kazem who escaped Iraq and arrived illegally in Britain around two years ago. He'd travelled through Europe, crossing the Channel, and was picked up when his boat got into trouble. He claimed asylum, but was refused. Due to be deported, he escaped the detention centre. It looks as though he's been living rough around here for some months, which explains the wolfman sightings. The immediate question for us is whether Hassan fits into our murder inquiry, or not? Dr Lane said he seemed to know Dax when he mentioned him, and we know that Dax was in a homosexual relationship at the time of his death.'

DI Painter paused and looked at the faces in front of him.

'So where has Hassan been living? He was illegal, so he couldn't have been renting on the open market.'

'Could Dax have been renting somewhere else?' DS Reid suggested.

'He wouldn't have had the funds for that and yet we suspect that Dax was spending time somewhere else. We could be looking at some kind of squat or maybe a farm outbuilding, any empty properties around the forest edges. I want to find where Hassan and possibly Dax were staying. It could have evidence which answers all our questions. Right, any other updates?'

'We know that it was definitely Dax who had the fight with Sam, thanks to CCTV, but it looks like Dax was the aggressor,' DC Gorman spoke up.

'So, where does that leave us with Sam? He might have been humiliated or angered by Dax and taken his revenge on him? But we also know Chester had an argument with Dax. So, what about the cupcakes business? Who was looking into that? It connects Sam and Chester, and the Holmes family employed Summer,' DI Painter continued.

'I was looking into that, sir,' DS Reid replied.

'Any financial irregularities?'

'Nothing obvious. It's a profitable business and they pay their taxes. Energy costs are high, but that's inevitable when you've got those ovens on 24/7, and it has a relatively low staff head-count as it's said to be highly automated.'

'Can you talk to some former staff, see if they've got any insights?'

'Sure, and there's one more thing, boss. I was looking through the CCTV from the firebombing of the developers that

Patrick had been arrested for. I reckon that one of the group was Sam Green. I recognised the hoodie: it was the same one he was wearing when we interviewed him.'

'Well, that is interesting. Sounds to me he's quite happy to break the law in more ways than one. I'm going to have another chat with Sam Green. We probably won't get a charge against him for the fight with Dax because he'll claim self-defence, but I'd like to see if he knew about Hassan. Any headway with the phones?'

'No sign of Summer's phone at her cottage and Dax's is still missing. However, the data from Summer's confirms that she did ring the Holmes house in the late afternoon before she was killed, which fits with what Phillip Holmes said about her calling in sick.'

'We need to track down these phones. If the killer has taken them then that suggests they may have evidence on them. Anyone not assigned, I want you all out there looking for where Hassan was living. I think if we can find that, then we may finally make some headway.'

35

'I expect you're going to tell me that there's no such thing as intuition and I need to stick to the facts and evidence,' DI Painter said to Harrison as the incident room briefing broke up. 'But I still think Chester Holmes is playing us. I want to go back and rattle his cage this afternoon, once I've spoken to Sam Green.'

'I think you're right,' Harrison agreed. 'And by the way, intuition is more than just a feeling. It's your lifetime's experience working in your subconscious. Your brain is finding the patterns in what you're seeing and using its knowledge to judge the situation. While your conscious mind is focusing on the big picture, it's working behind the scenes and usually faster, too.'

Painter hmphed. 'That for real?'

'Yes, it's been scientifically researched.'

'Wonder if I can intuitively pick the lottery numbers this week then? I'm going to give it a damned good go. That would give me a nice retirement.' Painter walked out of the incident room, chuckling.

Harrison was still convinced that the library book held the

key and so he picked it up and took another look. What was he looking for and how would he know when he'd found it?

'Is that the book you think Summer and Dax both read before they were killed?' DC Sally Gorman had walked up to Harrison.

'Yes. But if I'm honest, I'm struggling. I'm not from around here and so I can't tell what's unusual and what's not. It's a local walks guide from the 1970s.'

'Whoa, that's ancient. It's before I was born, but I grew up around here, so maybe I'd notice if something was around then but isn't now. Perhaps that's what they found out?' She smiled excitedly at him, eager to please.

'I'd be grateful if you would look through for me. I'm going to head out with DS Reid, help with the search for where Hassan may have been staying. If you find anything, please call immediately, no matter how insignificant it seems.'

It had started to rain again as Harrison and DS Freddie Reid left the station.

'Bloody weather. Like we haven't had enough rain already,' Freddie said to Harrison as they got into the car. 'The boss has asked us to concentrate the search on the eastern side of the forest, that's where most of the sightings have been. We're going to start the car park end and the other teams will work the areas towards the north. Besides the Bemford farm, there's a couple of others along that stretch.'

As they got underway, DS Reid suddenly changed the topic, glancing quickly at Harrison. 'Do you work out every day? I mean, you're pretty jacked.' He motioned to Harrison's muscles.

'I don't work out every day, but usually three times a week and I run most days, too.'

'I'm at the gym three times a week, but I'm nowhere near as pumped as you. Do you take supplements or something?'

'No,' Harrison replied. 'Just eat sensibly.'

'So what kind of routine do you do?'

They spent the rest of the journey running through Harrison's gym routine in detail before heading up a dirt track towards a large barn on the outskirts of the forest.

'Don't think this place is used anymore,' Freddie said, peering through the rain at the structure. It was a combination of dark green corrugated iron and brick. Harrison suspected it had once been used to store hay for the winter to feed cattle in the surrounding fields. They'd not seen any cows in the fields on the drive up so chances were as Freddie said, it was now disused.

The two men got out of the car, pulling their coat collars up to prevent the rain from dripping down their necks. They trod carefully on the squelchy mud so as not to end up sitting down in it. The big end doors to the barn were padlocked shut so they walked round the far side to check if there was another way in. Towards the end, they came across a door. DS Reid tried the handle and it opened. He glanced at Harrison. They were both hoping this was it.

The interior was dark with just shafts of light coming from small segments of clear corrugated plastic which acted as de facto windows. Dust filled the beams of light, giving movement to an otherwise still interior. At one end, a few hay bales were still piled up and as they got closer, the rustle of what were no doubt rats and field mice alerted them to the fact they weren't totally alone.

'I can't see that he's been staying here,' DS Reid said to Harrison.

The pair approached the bales to ensure there wasn't a hidden area behind.

'No,' Harrison replied, giving one last look around the interior. 'There's nowhere to hide.'

Their next visit was a small farm. The owners were an elderly couple and more than happy for them to look around.

'I don't think you'd be finding him here,' the elderly man said to them. 'All our buildings are used for one thing or another and we've not seen him about.'

They looked anyway, searching a barn in which DS Reid was delighted to find an old Morris Minor under a tarpaulin. Old farming machinery filled the rest of the barn. In another small outbuilding, empty crates told of a once busy farm.

DS Reid got on his police radio.

'Everyone's drawing blanks. We're going to have to widen the search area,' he relayed to Harrison. 'The DI said he'd also put a media call out in case anyone has been harbouring him.'

'Has anyone checked around the Bemford farm?'

'Not yet, but in all honesty I can't see that there's anywhere he could have been hiding without them knowing and I'm doubting that Chester and Phillip are the charitable type.' Freddie sighed. 'Yeah, I know, we've still got to look. No stone unturned and all that.'

DS Reid traipsed back to his car with Harrison in tow. The Bemford farm was just down the road from where they'd been so it only took minutes to arrive. The delicious waft of baking cupcakes being pumped out of the factory, met them as they arrived, along with Phillip Holmes.

'Chester isn't back yet if that's what you're here for,' he said to them defensively.

'Actually, Mr Holmes, it's not. We are conducting a search of all outbuildings in an effort to find where a man who might be connected with our enquiries has been staying.'

'You're looking for the wolfman, aren't you?' he said almost triumphantly, 'so you've finally realised that Chester has nothing to do with this and that vagrant is the murderer.'

'I didn't say that, no, Mr Holmes. I said that we were looking for a man who might be connected with our enquiries.'

'I heard he'd tried to break into a house on the Peacock estate last night,' Phillip added.

'We haven't received any such allegations, Mr Holmes. So, would it be possible to check all your outbuildings please?'

'Sure. I'll give you the tour. Let's start with the stables.'

Phillip Holmes led them across to the wooden stables. Harrison wasn't expecting to find anything here; he'd already looked that morning and there was nowhere for a man to hide, but he went along with the tour. It all looked the same as it had earlier.

'We've got a small shed out in the back garden and a garage round the side; we can look in those too, but I'm telling you that nobody has been staying there.'

They all duly walked around the house, looking in the shed that held nothing but gardening equipment, and then into the garage which was spotless and contained a Range Rover, a Mercedes, and a Porsche 911.

'That's it,' Phillip Holmes said to them, crossing his arms. 'We pulled all the other buildings down to build the factory, there's nowhere else.'

'What about the factory?' DS Reid asked.

'That's locked and in constant use. Of course there's not a bloody tramp staying there!' Phillip Holmes guffawed.

'I'm sure you also appreciate that it would be good for us to ensure we've checked everywhere. I can't go back to my boss and say we didn't look around the factory. Well, I could but...' DS Reid left his sentence hanging, making it clear that he could seek additional police powers if required.

'Fine. But you'll have to wear protective clothing if we go inside. This is a food production facility. We have to maintain the highest hygiene standards.'

'Let's walk around the perimeter first,' Freddie suggested. 'Make sure there's no access points.'

'This is a modern building, highly regulated, there are no access points where vagrants can take shelter,' Phillip was incredulous.

DS Reid ignored him and set off walking around the factory building. Harrison followed, fully aware that the DS was at least in part playing this totally by the book in order to irritate Phillip Holmes. His attitude towards the man whom they now knew to be Hassan hadn't gone down well with either of them.

Apart from a fire exit which was locked from the outside, there were no potential entry points into the factory and the main doors were also key card protected.

'Forest is basically on your doorstep,' Freddie said nodding towards the thick mass of trees which almost butted up to the far end of the factory. 'And you say you saw a man with dark hair in the trees a few times?'

'Yes. Chester also said he'd seen him in the woods sometimes when they went riding.'

'Any idea of the direction he went in? Was there a specific area that he seemed to stick to?' Freddie asked.

Phillip shook his head.

'OK, well, I don't see much point in checking inside the factory, it's all locked. We'll be on our way. What time did you say that Chester was back?'

'In the next hour,' Phillip replied.

'Well that was a total waste of time, apart from irritating the grumpy sod. Still not offered us a cupcake!' DS Reid slumped into the driver's seat of his car. 'Where the hell was Hassan living?'

'Why don't we go back to where we know he definitely was, the area that he appeared on the drone footage. I might be able to find some tracks that will indicate which direction and where he came from.'

'Seriously? In this weather?'

'The weather won't help but if he has a regular route then that might be more obvious.'

DS Reid huffed. 'I mean, what's the point, honestly? We know there are no structures in the woods. We're going to get soaked for nothing.'

'If he enters the woods by the same route then it could tell us in what area or direction we need to concentrate. I don't mind going alone if you want to stay in the car,' Harrison said to him.

DS Reid considered it for a moment. 'No, I'd better come. Won't look great if the boss discovers I'm sitting on my arse in the car while you hunt around.'

Even Harrison had to admit it wasn't an overly pleasant task. The trees seemed to save up the largest droplets of rainwater to release straight down the back of their necks as they passed underneath. The ground was sodden, making their feet cold and damp, and the visibility wasn't exactly great.

'My bloody socks are wet now,' DS Reid moaned behind Harrison.

'I think we're close to where he first appeared on the drone footage,' Harrison said to him, ignoring his endless string of complaints about the weather.

'We can't be far from the Holmes's section of the woods again.'

As if answering DS Reid's comment, the two men started to see signs nailed onto trees that said, *Keep Out Private Property* or *Trespassers will be prosecuted CCTV in use.*

'They weren't joking when they said they didn't like the public going into their woods,' Reid said. 'But I certainly can't see anywhere that Hassan could have been sheltering around here. No magical gingerbread cottage.'

Harrison stopped and let the detective stomp off away from him until his moaning became more of a mumble. Then he calmed his mind and prepared to focus. All he could see were trees still. From here he couldn't quite see the Bemford cupcake factory, but he knew it wasn't far. He thought about Hassan, walking through the trees heading towards the clearing.

Finally, Harrison turned his attention to the ground. It would be hard to find any tracks from Hassan – almost impossible to know if they were his or someone else's – but he might get lucky. He started scanning the forest floor as he heard DS Reid come stomping back towards him.

'There's nothing. This is a waste of time.'

'Have you seen any evidence of a path?' Harrison asked.

'No. Just trees and more bloody trees.'

If Harrison was honest, he was beginning to appreciate DS Reid's scepticism.

'Give me a bit more time,' he replied, continuing to scan the ground for any signs that someone had regularly walked across it.

DS Reid's mobile rang and so he stopped and answered it.

A minute later, he caught up with Harrison.

'That was Sally. Apparently, Patrick Sheldon's Land Rover was spotted on CCTV during a break in at a building site. Same development as the one where they firebombed the offices. Machinery was sabotaged and destroyed. There's an arrest warrant out for him. When they catch up with him we need to check his tyres with the tracks found in the car park following Summer's murder.'

Harrison was about to comment when he started to see signs where someone had regularly passed through.

'Someone comes this way,' he said to Freddie, who had been standing under a tree watching him, trying to keep out the rain. The detective walked over to where he was indicating.

'Yeah, even I see that.'

It wasn't a path, but the forest floor had been scuffed and trodden on enough for it to be obvious that a person, or people, had regularly passed over it.

Freddie scanned the area and walked straight towards a large clump of ferns.

'Dr Lane!' he shouted, 'over here.' He was picking a large branch up and tossed it aside.

Harrison ran over to where DS Reid was peering into the ferns, just inside the area of the woods owned by the Holmes family. His stomach did a flip. In front of them, right in the centre of the ferns, was a rusty round hatch.

'There were a couple of branches over it so I nearly missed it,' DS Reid said. 'What is it?'

'I'm not sure, it looks like some kind of underground shelter, and if someone has gone to some effort to hide it, then it could explain why Hassan just appears and disappears in the forest.'

'We're going to need to check and see if it is, and not just a cesspit or water storage tank. I think we're on the Holmes's land here.'

Harrison shrugged. 'It's a murder inquiry. There could be another victim down there.'

Freddie stepped closer to the hatch and pulled it open carefully, as though something might spring out of it and attack him. There was a metal ladder which led down into the ground. He got his phone out and used the light to peer inside.

'It's dry. I can see a concrete floor but it's too dark to see what else is in there. We're going to have to go down to check.' He stood back up as though deciding what to do next.

'You want me to go first?' Harrison asked.

'If you like,' DS Reid replied, trying not to show his relief.

Harrison grasped the metal ladder, giving it a small shake to test its robustness, before stepping on the rungs and beginning the descent.

It was pitch black inside, not surprisingly, and so he'd stopped after a few rungs to get his phone torch out. He had no idea what he was descending into. He could see the concrete floor that Freddie had mentioned, and as he got lower, a room or chamber began to be illuminated. There was a mattress on the floor as a bed and some other pieces of furniture, but it was what was on the walls which told the full story.

'This is it,' he shouted up to Freddie, 'this is where Hassan was staying – and Dax too.'

'I'll call it in,' DS Reid's disembodied voice came from above.

Harrison continued down to the bottom, and then stood at the base of the ladder and scanned the room.

It was a perfect little hideaway with everything that Hassan had needed. Candles littered the room, clearly his method of light, and there was a small Calor gas camping stove. A plastic thermal ice box was on the floor and Harrison suspected they might find some of the missing sheep inside. Despite his dire circumstances, Hassan had made an effort to make it feel like a home, and that thought alone brought a wave of sadness for the man who had chosen to take his own life rather than be returned to his homeland.

But it was on the walls that Harrison saw the tragic story of Hassan and Dax's relationship. There were photographs of the two of them, smiling and happy, but the majority of the wall was taken up with a battle plan to get Hassan's extradition order appealed and enable him to claim asylum. It told of a bright young man, persecuted and tortured, and of Dax's efforts to find a legal route to help him. It was a collage of love and hope. Hassan had clearly spent weeks if not months down here, living in a dark hole in the ground hidden from the sun and yet here he and Dax had found happiness together.

'Bloody hell,' DS Reid exclaimed. He'd started down the ladder and was scanning the room with his phone light. 'What the hell is this place?' Freddie added.

'I'm not sure. It's some kind of shelter or storage facility. Dax must have been bringing him supplies and water.' Harrison had already noted the camping water barrel, which was by a kettle and plastic washing bowl. Then he looked over every wall.

'There are no doors into another section. It's just a room on its own. Perhaps someone built it as a bomb or nuclear shelter years ago and forgot about it. It's definitely relatively modern.'

'I can't see anything that links to the Vikings or runes,' DS Reid said, thinking aloud. 'But certainly looks like this was where Dax used to spend time with Hassan. Those are some of his forest bathing leaflets. We'd better get back up top, we need forensics to comb the place.'

Harrison nodded. He'd not wanted to contaminate anything which was why he'd stayed at the bottom of the ladder, but before he went back up, he took a few photographs of the wall and the room. Then, he climbed back up the metal ladder to the circle of light and the forest. Freddie was on his phone talking to the office.

As he reached the surface again, his own mobile pinged. It was a message saying that he'd missed a call. He rang the messaging service.

'Dr Lane, it's DC Gorman. Sally. You were right about the book. I think I know what it was that Dax and Summer found. The book mentions a big underground shelter complex at the edge of the woods built in the 1960s during the Cold War. It's been totally forgotten about. I've never heard of it and it's not on any maps. We think that must be where Hassan was hiding. I've told DI Painter and he's on his way back. He couldn't find Sam Green: he's missing. Nobody has seen him since he left custody and his lawyer can't get hold of him.'

DS Reid finished his call and turned to Harrison. 'Sam Green's gone missing. That's Sam and Patrick now AWOL.'

'Yes, Sally called,' Harrison replied. 'She also said that the book Dax and Summer read shows a big underground Cold War shelter complex.'

DS Reid looked nonplussed. 'Well, I wouldn't call it much of a complex. It's just one room.'

Harrison looked over Freddie's shoulder at the silhouette of the Bemford Cupcake factory building behind him.

'What if that is just a tiny part of it? What if the main complex is underneath the cupcake factory?'

There was silence as the two men both contemplated what that could mean.

'They must know that, surely? They wouldn't have been able to build the factory without discovering the shelter?' Freddie said.

'Definitely.'

'So what would they be using it for?' Reid thought out loud again. 'That doesn't fit with state-of-the-art modern hygiene standards.'

'Exactly.'

36

When Harrison and DS Reid walked up to the front of the Holmes's farmhouse, the place seemed eerily quiet.

'Where is everyone?' Reid said, searching around. 'That's Sam Green's moped. I recognise it from watching the CCTV footage.'

Harrison looked over to where Freddie was pointing. Sam's moped was parked in front of the house and not where he'd have expected it to be, outside the factory in the staff parking area.

Reid knocked on the front door, ominously remarking, 'No greeting party from Phillip today.'

They waited, but nobody came to the door.

Then, at the same time, they both heard the sound of crying. DS Reid looked at Harrison to see if he'd heard it, too, then knocked again.

'It's coming from the sitting room. They must be able to hear us knocking,' Freddie commented.

Harrison reached out and tried the door handle. It opened.

'Mrs Holmes? Mr Holmes? It's DS Reid and Dr Lane. Is everything alright?' Reid called out.

The crying was far from light, coming in gut-wrenching sobs.

'I'm going in,' Freddie said to Harrison. 'Mrs Holmes?' he called again as he walked cautiously into the sitting room.

Dawn Holmes was kneeling on the floor by the sprawled body of her husband. Blood oozed from several wounds on Phillip's chest and body. His eyes stared vacantly at the ceiling.

'Code one. DS Reid, urgent assistance required. One male seriously wounded. Unknown attacker. Bemford Farm. Sam Green's moped on the premises.'

Harrison approached Dawn Holmes and crouched down to her eye level. The woman was clearly distraught. She was rocking backwards and forwards, holding on to her dead husband's hand, and sobbing uncontrollably, almost unaware that they were in the room.

'Mrs Holmes,' he said calmly. 'Mrs Holmes. Who did this?'

There was no response. It was almost as if she hadn't heard him.

He reached out to feel Phillip's neck for a pulse. Although every instinct in him said that life had left the man already, he needed to be sure. He felt nothing.

'Mrs Holmes, did Sam Green do this?' Harrison tried. 'Is Chester back?'

She lifted her eyes to him at her son's name.

'It's my fault. I shouldn't have told him.'

'Shouldn't have told who what, Mrs Holmes?' Harrison asked. 'Told Chester?'

She shook her head.

Behind him, DS Reid relayed the need for armed backup. Whoever had stabbed Phillip could still be on site and dangerous.

'It's my fault. He wouldn't have done this if...' She trailed off, staring at her husband's lifeless face.

'What is your fault, Mrs Holmes?' Harrison pushed.

Dawn Holmes just shook her head again and carried on sobbing and rocking.

Harrison stood back up. He wasn't going to get any information from Dawn Holmes in the foreseeable future, and there was nothing anyone could do for Phillip.

'Sam could be anywhere,' Freddie said to him. 'We should wait for armed backup. If he's lost it, then he's going to be dangerous.'

'What about the factory workers? They could be in danger,' Harrison said to him.

DS Reid thought for a moment. 'OK, let's check and see if they're alright and get them evacuated.'

He turned and ran from the house towards the factory, Harrison alongside him.

The second they got there, Reid tried to open the door. 'It's unlocked!' He pulled the door open and walked in cautiously. 'Police. Is anyone inside?'

Nothing.

The interior of the factory looked empty.

'I can't see anyone,' Freddie said. 'Where are they all? I thought this place was 24/7?'

'There are no other vehicles here either,' Harrison added, looking out the side windows at the staff car park. 'Someone has sent the staff home.'

'We need to check the offices,' Freddie nodded towards the end of the factory where a door carried the sign, *Office*.

The door was also unlocked and they walked in cautiously.

'Police show yourselves,' Freddie shouted. 'What's that smell?' Freddie exclaimed as he opened the door. A pungent aroma hit them both, along with a humid wave of warm air that was at odds with the controlled environment of the factory.

'That's marijuana,' Freddie answered his own question. The smell unmistakable.

In front of them was an office which filled around half the width of the factory. The smell was coming from an open door that looked as though it led to a stationery cupboard.

'I think we've just found what they use the underground shelter for,' Reid said, heading straight for the cupboard door. 'We'd better go carefully though as I've seen some nasty booby traps in these places before.'

DS Reid quickly updated his colleagues via his police radio and got an estimated time of arrival for backup.

'The cupcakes must be just a front, all those deliveries they're doing, they're delivering drugs not bloody cakes.'

'That explains the mystery of why Sam can afford that flat,' Harrison added.

The two of them had walked cautiously into the large stationery cupboard, where a trap door in the floor had been carelessly discarded and left open. Steps led down into a brightly lit underground cavern. Reid walked down warily, and Harrison followed.

'Police. Is anyone down here? Come out now with your hands raised.'

The two of them came to a stop at the bottom of the steps and listened. Silence.

'It's bloody huge!' Freddie exclaimed.

As far as they could see, there were cannabis plants. The entire place was packed with them, and the wires and tubes that were needed for the growing process criss-crossed the ceilings and floor.

'There's probably more rooms than just this one too,' Harrison said, beginning to feel slightly sick with the strong smell and warm humidity.

'You're right. I think we should go back up and wait for

backup. We've no idea who or what is down here. They could well be armed. This is big money.'

'Look,' Harrison nodded at the wall. Someone had drawn what looked like a large upward pointing arrow on the wall.

'An arrow?' Freddie asked.

'I don't think that's an arrow. I think it's the warrior rune, the Norse god of justice, Tyr, often inscribed on battle weapons.'

'That's the same symbol that was on the spear used against Dax.'

'Yes, and I also think that might be blood that's it's been painted with.'

'Right, well I definitely don't fancy a spear through my guts, so let's get back up top and wait for the armed backup.' DS Reid started back up the steps.

Harrison was relieved to get outside in the fresh air. The atmosphere in the shelter was stifling and he pulled clean, cool air into his lungs deeply to re-oxygenate his body.

'I bet Sam's long gone,' Freddie said. 'Do you think he's been running this whole outfit?'

'I'm not so sure about that,' Harrison replied. 'He's definitely involved but then so too must be Chester and Phillip.'

'So, who's the killer? Sam or Chester?'

Just then, a noise over at the stable block made both men turn. Within seconds, they were running across the front of the house straight towards it.

As they got to the side of the stables, caution made them both stop and listen. For a few seconds, all they could hear was their own breathing as their lungs caught up with the need to receive oxygenated blood. Then there was the sound of munching. A horse slowly walked out from behind the stables and across the grass. It had its bridle on, but the reins were trailing on the floor. It was eating grass.

'One of the horses is out of its box,' Harrison whispered.

'I know I can see it,' Reid replied.

'No. I can hear hooves on concrete, there's another one besides that one.'

'Police. Come out now with your hands where we can see them,' the detective shouted.

Harrison craned to hear something, anything. He was about to suggest that he went around the other side while Reid remained in position, when they heard a groan.

'Someone's injured…' Reid edged towards the corner of the stable block to peer round it. 'They're lying on the ground. I can see feet,' he added and stepped forward from behind the stable block.

Harrison's reflexes were fast. His arm shot out and grabbed the back of DS Reid's suit, yanking him back towards him and behind the stable block, just as a whistling sound flew by, followed by a thud.

Freddie crashed back into Harrison, who was staring at the spear which had missed the young detective by inches and was now embedded in a large blue water butt that was slowly leaking its contents.

For a few moments, the detective was speechless as he watched the water pooling on the floor.

He didn't have time to react: the sound of a horse's clattering hooves came towards them. The killer wasn't waiting for them to try that move again. At the same time, Harrison became aware of the siren heading up the drive.

'We can't outrun him,' he now said. 'Come round here. Backup is coming.'

They turned and hid round the other corner, flattening themselves against the back of the stables, just as the horseman appeared and clattered along where they'd both just been standing seconds ago. They heard him urge the pony on with a roar and then he careered past the two men, running straight at the unmarked police car, which had arrived in the yard, and its driver and passenger who were getting out and walking towards the house.

The rider had on a full-face horned metal Viking helmet, an animal skin over his shoulders, and carried a huge axe in his right hand. He was on one of the polo ponies, steering with his left hand and urging it on with his legs. And he was heading straight for DI Painter and DC Sally Gorman.

The two detectives had already got out of the car before they clocked the incoming threat. The armed response unit hadn't arrived yet and they were defenceless.

'Run!' DI Painter shouted to Sally, who was rooted to the spot in disbelief at what she was seeing.

Painter ran back towards the car. The rider let out a roar and rode straight at Sally, raising the axe, ready to strike. Finally, her survival instinct kicked in and she broke into a run. But she wasn't thinking; she was panicking. Instead of running into the house or back to the car, she ran straight across the front lawn.

The killer turned the pony on the spot and followed her, still roaring, waving the axe above his head.

Harrison had already wrenched the spear out of the water butt, and was now running along the side of the lawn, diagonally to Sally. She would cross his path, and so, too, would the horse. If he ran fast enough.

He put everything he had into his sprint, but watched in horror as Sally slipped on the wet grass and fell spread-eagled on the lawn. The rider was almost upon her now, the horse in full gallop.

She scrambled back onto her feet and carried on running, her eyes wide with fear.

Harrison stopped as Sally ran across his path about twenty or so yards away from him. He rooted himself to the ground. Anger was burning deep inside him. Anger at the man who was running Sally down like an animal. Anger at the fact he'd no doubt already taken innocent lives.

He was not going to take Sally's.

Harrison heaved his powerful biceps and shoulder muscles back, reaching behind him with the spear. He would get only one chance to save her. There were split seconds to judge the speed of the horse with the speed of the spear.

He threw.

The spear whistled through the air on a collision course with the pony and rider. Harrison watched it in slow motion, willing it to find its target.

It missed.

The spear landed in the ground just in front of them.

The pony turned fast, spooked by the spear.

Sally had disappeared from sight around the far end of the stables and the sound of several police sirens tearing up the driveway caused the rider to spin his horse around. He saw them, knew that he was now massively outnumbered and with another roar, urged the pony on towards the forest.

Harrison didn't hesitate. He ran back to the stables, where the loose horse was still grazing. He grabbed its reins and vaulted onto its back.

'What are you doing?' Reid shouted at him. 'There's no saddle.'

'I've never ridden with one,' Harrison replied, 'he's not getting away.' He urged the horse into a gallop and headed off in the same direction as the Viking rider.

It had been a while since Harrison had ridden and the horse wasn't used to him, or being ridden bare back so it was skittish as they made their way across the short area of grass towards the forest. At one point it tried a little buck, but Harrison wasn't going anywhere. He needed to track where the Viking rider went so they could arrest him.

As they arrived at the trees, Harrison slowed the horse down.

There wasn't a path so the horse needed to pick its way more carefully through the debris of the forest floor. Thankfully, the rain had stopped but it was still very wet underfoot and it would be easy to slip. Although the Viking rider had a good head start on him, he could just see him up ahead through the trees. He too had slowed right down. Harrison pulled his phone from his pocket and called DI Painter.

'He's heading west, towards the main path that leads to the clearing,' he said to him.

'Harrison, do not try to apprehend. He is armed and dangerous. We have armed support on their way to the forest car park now.'

Harrison didn't reply. He was focusing on the rider up ahead. He left his phone line open, slipping it back into his pocket so he could give updates as he went. Harrison let the horse pick its way through the forest, trusting in the animal to keep its footing, while being careful that he didn't get knocked off his horse by a low tree branch. He didn't take his eyes off his target, who appeared to have stopped and had his head bowed, possibly texting or sending a message on his mobile phone. It allowed Harrison to get closer. Close enough that the Viking rider heard him approach as Harrison's horse clonked a log with its hoof.

With the warning sound, the rider was off again, spurring his pony forward and onto the wide path which ran between the car park and the clearing. Now he could really increase the speed. For a few seconds it looked as though he might turn left towards the car park, but instead he swung right.

It took Harrison a little longer to get through the dense forest and reach the path. He'd relayed the update to DI Painter, and then he too urged his horse into a gallop up the wide path in pursuit.

Harrison's horse was steady and fast; the Viking, however, was riding the polo pony with the injured leg and his pace was slowing considerably. If he stopped for a moment to think,

Harrison wasn't sure what he would do if and when he caught up with him. He wasn't a good enough horseman to outmanoeuvre him with acrobatics, and he didn't like the idea of being hit by an axe, but he also wasn't about to let the man get out of his sight. Overhead in the distance, Harrison could hear the rotor blades of a helicopter. DI Painter must have called it in to help with tracking them.

As they grew closer to the clearing, the Viking became more agitated, kicking at the pony to get it to go faster. Harrison had no idea what was on the other side of the clearing; did the path continue, or would they be back into dense forest?

Harrison arrived at the entrance to the clearing as the Viking was about to reach the other side. He turned round to see where Harrison was, a look of sheer determination in his eyes. He wasn't about to give up.

Only he didn't have an option.

The Viking turned back round in the direction he was going too late. The pony had run underneath a thick long branch of the yew tree, but there was only enough clearance for the horse. Harrison heard the crack as the branch hit the man's head and helmet.

The rider fell to the floor with a huge thump. His helmet fell from his head and his axe slid across the clearing, out of his reach. The pony carried on for a few moments before realising it was no longer being kicked, and it came to a halt.

Harrison and his mount finished the last twenty feet and he jumped down to see how badly the man was injured. He was out cold, lying face down on the forest floor.

'I have him. We need an ambulance, he's hit his head on a tree,' Harrison barked to DI Painter. He felt for a pulse. He was still alive.

Harrison rolled the man over onto his back and looked at the pale face of Chester Holmes. Blood trickled down his forehead from a gash on his head. The Viking helmet had obviously not been genuine, just like its wearer, because it had provided no protection from the blow. Harrison put him into the recovery position, concerned he might swallow his own tongue, and then sat on the damp forest floor monitoring his breathing and pulse, and waiting for the paramedics.

Beside them was the yew tree. Silent and majestic. Dax's photographs were still pinned to its trunk, his smiling face looking out at the clearing and the man who was most probably his killer. Harrison couldn't help thinking that it was divine justice that Chester had run into the tree. The forest and the yew that Dax had loved so much had taken its revenge for him. Justice had indeed been served.

37

Chester Holmes had concussion and a case of severely dented macho pride, but he was discharged from hospital after twenty-four hours. He left his medical bed for one in a cell and was charged with two counts of murder and one of attempted murder.

Harrison hadn't needed to wait long in the clearing. Firearms officers had arrived quickly and as soon as they were happy that the threat had been neutralised, the paramedics and rest of the murder investigation team, were allowed in.

'Bloody hell!' DI Painter had exclaimed breathlessly as he found Harrison collecting the two horses who had wandered to the edges of the clearing and were viewing proceedings warily.

'How's Sam Green?' Harrison had asked him.

'He'll be fine. He took a spear in the gut but the doctors say it's not life threatening. He came round as the paramedics were taking him away. Told us a few interesting stories. We've got a team in the underground cannabis factory – looks like you were right about that book being the trigger. Dax must have been wondering what the shelter was that Hassan had found. Or perhaps he suspected what was really going on at the Bemford

Cupcake factory. Either way, he found the evidence of its existence in that book and confronted Chester with it and tried to blackmail him. Said he needed the money to help a friend. I'm guessing that friend was Hassan.'

'On the wall in Hassan's room, there was a list of lawyers and also organisations like Asylum Aid and Right to Remain. Patrick told me Dax had been looking for a job too and Summer said he wanted to study law. He was doing all he could to help keep Hassan in the UK.'

'Tragic but unfortunately Chester Holmes was not the charitable type. Sam said Dax also confronted him about the drugs and being in Chester's pocket. That's what caused their bust up. We'll interview Chester as soon as he's well enough.'

'Is DC Gorman alright?'

Tony Painter smiled. 'She's fine. A bit wobbly legged after nearly being run down by an axe-wielding Viking. She can certainly say that her first murder case was an interesting one.'

'I'll take these two horses back to the stables. We'll have to arrange for someone to look after them as I doubt Mrs Holmes is going to be available.'

'No. She's already in the custody suite. We're being sensitive as she's lost her husband, but she's still an accessory to what must be a drugs business that's been making millions, and to murder. That makes her a serious flight risk.'

'So, did Phillip kill Summer?' Harrison asked.

DI Painter nodded. 'Dawn Holmes said he never liked her. Used to get very angry when Summer used her natural medicines on the horses and then he found out that Chester and she were having a relationship. As we know, she did ring that afternoon before she was murdered, but it was to speak to Chester. She'd found out about the shelter and wanted to know if it was him who had murdered Dax. He'd denied it but they knew she didn't believe him and they were convinced she was going to tell us. While Chester went up to London, Phillip decided that they had to silence her. They went round to Summer's cottage and it was Dawn who drove Summer's car to the woods. She said she sat in their car while Phillip took her into the trees, and then they'd gone back to her cottage and cleared up as much evidence of their son as possible. They knew Chester had an alibi because he was up in London. Thing was, they miscalculated. Chester apparently did really like Summer. Went crazy apparently and stabbed his father when he got home and realised what they'd done. What I don't get is the Viking outfit!'

'Summer and Chester were two opposites. She connected with the spiritual side of her Norse heritage. He revelled in the macho glory of the stories of raiders who just did what they wanted and took what they wanted,' Harrison said sadly. 'It fed into his ego. Phillip knew nothing about runes hence his rudimentary attempts to copy them onto Summer in order to make us think it was the same killer and therefore take Chester out of the frame for both murders as he wasn't here.'

'To be fair, it worked to an extent. It was only you who saw through that one,' DI Painter added with a sigh.

As Harrison slowly led the two horses home, the polo pony limping after the treatment he'd had from Chester, the full extent of the police operation was laid out in front of him. The house and factory were surrounded by police and forensics vehicles. They would be there for days, if not weeks more.

As he approached the stables, DC Gorman and DS Reid spotted him and walked across.

'Are you alright?' Harrison asked Sally.

She nodded. 'I was stupid. I panicked.'

'Hard not to when you've got a crazy Viking on horseback heading at you with an axe,' Reid said to her reassuringly. 'I think I'd have shat my pants if I'm honest.'

Sally smiled at him and shook her head. For once, she appreciated Freddie's humour.

Harrison felt for the young woman who was just beginning to see the extent of what people were prepared to do for money, love, and just sheer power. It had turned out to be quite a first case for the new detective, but the energy that was in her eyes told him she was definitely only just beginning.

'They've got Patrick,' DS Reid said to Harrison, 'he was picked up heading for Dover. Not a bad haul for one day's work – oh, and thanks for the timely intervention earlier,' he looked slightly sheepish, 'glad I didn't get skewered.' He smiled.

Harrison smiled back. 'You're welcome.'

Back at the horses' stalls, Harrison gently took off their bridles and the rest of the tack from the polo pony. Then, he gave them each a net of hay and picked up a brush. Slowly, rhythmically he started to groom them, brushing the dust and forest from their coats. He wasn't sure who got the most therapy out of it – him or the horses. He could have stayed in the stables for at least another hour, allowing the stress and tragedy of the last few days to slowly seep from him, but DS Reid had arranged for some-body to take him back to the station where he could pick up his bike.

Just as he was about to leave, Harrison looked up. In the gap between the roof and the walls of the wooden structure, was something silver. He got up closer to look and realised it was the hammer of Thor; a symbol of both good and bad, it represented protection, blessings, but was also used as a devastating weapon. An object worn as a talisman by Norsemen and now modern heathens. It had probably been put there by Summer to keep the horses safe. Phillip had clearly missed it. Harrison wondered how long it would stay there, a tiny legacy of Summer's heritage and beliefs.

. . .

Harrison had returned to the station to pick up his bike, but before he went back to the hotel to checkout he wanted to do something. He looked at the images on Dax's phone which the investigators had found in Hassan's room, and took some photographs of his own. Then, he went into town where he printed them out.

Next, he took one final trip to the forest car park and walked up the path to the yew tree clearing. When he got there, he was alone. All signs of the chaos of earlier had gone, the wind chimes the only sounds in the air. Mournful and sad, they tinkled and clanked in the breeze, with the gentle whisper of the trees as an accompaniment.

Harrison took out the three photographs he'd had printed. One of Summer, smiling at the camera, one of Dax and Hassan, arms around each other's shoulders, and one of the three of them. A selfie of three young faces all laughing at the camera, captured in a moment that was lost. Forever young.

He pinned the photographs to the yew tree trunk next to the pictures of Dax. It felt right to do this. As though they all somehow belonged to the tree. Harrison had begun the week looking at the yew as the tree of death, and it had been at the centre of two tragic losses, but not through any fault of its own. It seemed like their three souls were now entwined within it. It had taken their life essence and made them a part of its never-ending life cycle.

Perhaps he was getting soft in his old age, or maybe it was the emotions brought on by his dilemma with Tanya, but the strength of the love between Dax and Hassan – a relationship that had survived despite all the odds – and their friendship with the young woman who loved the trees as much as they did, deserved some recognition. They had tried to take care of the woodland. They had believed in Yggdrasil, the sacred Norse tree from which all life had come, and so it was right that it now took care of them.

38

For a man who had been desperate to head back home, Harrison spent every moment of his journey to London filled with dread. He'd left the team to mop up the aftermath of Chester's drugs empire. The National Crime Agency had sent specialist drugs officers after they'd discovered just how big the old shelter under the factory was. The Holmes' cake business didn't make anywhere near the number of cupcakes that they declared on their accounts, but it had hidden the extent of their energy costs needed to grow the plants and provided the perfect cover for deliveries.

It was going to take a big investigation to try to unpick the network that Chester had built up. His parents had been willing accomplices to the plan, as it had turned their fortunes around and prevented bankruptcy. Unfortunately, it had also created a monster.

The rain had started again, and it was tiring riding the bike in those conditions, but especially after the day Harrison had been through. He stopped at a motorway service station and even contemplated getting a coffee. In the end he settled for some noodles and a sparkling water. He might be wet outside, soaked through from the rain, but his body needed to rehydrate.

Sitting in the bright lights of the catering area, he watched people going about their business. Families rushing children to a toilet break, couples trying to decide what it was they were going to eat, lone drivers sitting staring at the families and the couples. Would he always be that lone driver at a service station?

He'd already texted Tanya to see if she was going to be in later. He'd made the decision to get it over and done with as soon as possible – the thought of the confrontation was chewing him up inside. He didn't want to say goodbye to her, but he thought it was the best he could do for her. He hoped that her own self-preservation would make it easier, that she'd agree and that would be that. He could ride back to his apartment and carry on with his life. He wanted to make it as easy as possible on Tanya and so he'd said he'd go round to her flat, see her on her own home territory.

Harrison scrunched flat the plastic bottle that had contained his water and got up to put it in the recycling bin. For a few moments, his thoughts were interrupted by the memory of a young woman, her eyes looking up at him, passionate about the environment and adamant that everyone had to do more than just recycle their waste. Summer had been right. Next time he'd ask for tap water in a cup and cut out the plastic altogether. His heart still felt sad for the young lives that had been wasted so needlessly in the past week. Every death, every murder was a loss, and he mourned each one of them.

Harrison was relieved to get back to his flat, but had to fight the overwhelming urge to just shower and go to bed. He imagined Hassan hiding away from the world in his underground bunker room. In there, he'd have felt safe. Here, Harrison felt safe. He didn't want to go and see Tanya and change the course of his life. He wanted things to stay just the way they were.

Harrison had one thing to be thankful for as he rode across London from Docklands to Fulham: it had stopped raining and after his shower, he felt more like himself. It didn't help his stomach, though, which had twisted into a thousand knots of apprehension.

Tanya always took his breath away when he saw her. She opened her flat door to him, the light from behind illuminating her long brunette hair. She smiled, but he noticed that the smile didn't light up her eyes like it usually did. Neither did she give him an excited hug and a kiss, her usual greeting.

Their meeting was awkward. Like two teenagers going on a first date, both of them holding back. He could see the apprehension in her face and the tight muscles of her body. Did she suspect something, or was she about to help him with his dilemma and steal the march on him? It was such a contrast to the way they had parted.

'How did it all go this week?' she asked, walking into her kitchen and pouring herself a large glass of red wine. 'What do you want to drink?'

'Just water, thanks. It wasn't a total success. Three murders and one suicide. I wasn't on top form, but we got the killers, eventually,' he replied.

Tanya sighed, which was unlike her, and said nothing else. She walked to the fridge and got out a large bottle of sparkling water, pouring him a glass.

'OK,' she said as she handed it to him. 'Do you want to tell me what's going on?'

Harrison was surprised by her sudden defensive tone. She'd put her wine down and kept the kitchen counter between them. Her face had lost its softness and was rigid and angry.

'We have a great long weekend, then I don't hear from you for days and I get this.' She picked up the card from the flowers and flung it onto the countertop in front of him.

'I'm sorry, I'm not sure what you mean.'

'I'm talking about these.' She opened her bin and Harrison saw the bouquet of roses, still wrapped, crushed inside. 'Who sent them, and why?'

'Who?' Harrison said, surprised.

'Yes. Who? I know they weren't from you. So, are you going to tell me what's going on?'

This had not been what he'd rehearsed or expected. He was lost for words.

Tanya was in full flow. 'I contacted the florists. They were bought by a man who came into their shop and gave cash. He had a baseball cap on. I've got the footage, but it's difficult to see who he is.' Tanya crossed her arms and looked at him defiantly. 'Why would some strange man send me flowers? He clearly doesn't know you well because you wouldn't have said that on the card, anyway.'

'It's a threat,' he rushed out. 'I'm sorry. Whoever it was that killed my mother has told me to stop investigating. They sent me photographs of us at the hotel last weekend. They followed you home, and then this.' He indicated the flower card. 'We're going to have to stop seeing each other. If you're with me, you're in danger.' He'd said it, finally got the words out in one big gush.

'Don't you dare play that card with me!' Tanya hit back. She was angry now. Incandescent.

Harrison was shocked. He'd expected her to be upset and tearful.

'Neither you, nor they, will make me a victim, and you have absolutely no right to see me as one. You've got to stop fighting the world on your own, Harrison Lane, and quit thinking only you can save everyone. I joined the police force to help fight the bad guys, too, and so I know exactly what drives you. But every murder is not your responsibility. This' – she stabbed at the card again – 'is not just on your shoulders. If you dare, for one minute, to allow them to threaten us, threaten me, and stop us from living our lives, then you should be ashamed of yourself.

Your mother came back to fight for something. Something she clearly thought was worth the risk. I've no intention of being another one of their victims, so if you seriously think you can just take the easy way out, dump me and walk out of here back to your Lone Ranger existence, then you have got another thing coming.'

He stared at her. Hot tears were pricking at the back of his eyes, and he couldn't find the words to respond to the beautiful, angry woman in front of him. She wasn't finished.

'If you can honestly stand there and tell me that you don't love me, you don't want to be with me, and you cannot see a future for us, then fine. Walk out the door. I will accept that. But if you're here to tell me that I'm better off without you, then you can shove that, because I can make my own mind up as to what I want to do and what is and isn't good for me.'

Harrison stepped forward and leaned on the counter. His heart and soul had been stripped bare by the words of the woman he knew he loved. 'I don't know what I'd do if something happened to you,' he stuttered out.

Tanya's anger disappeared, and her face softened. She reached out for his hand. 'We're a team, Harrison. We face this together.'

She came round from the other side of the counter and gently brushed away the tears that were coursing down his face.

'I love you,' he whispered.

39

Harrison slept until midday, wrapped and cocooned next to the woman he loved. The emotional and physical exhaustion of the past week had poured out of him. They'd talked for hours and he'd finally been completely honest with her, sharing his fears and his insecurities. She'd taken them all and wrapped them up in cotton wool for him, squeezing the poison from their bellies.

Together, they had come up with a plan. A way to continue the fight that his mother had started.

A couple of days later, Harrison and Tanya went to visit Professor Andrew McKendrick, his old mentor and friend. Andrew was delighted to hear from Harrison, and invited them both to lunch.

'I am honoured to meet the woman who has finally tamed Harrison's wild heart,' he laughed, giving Tanya's hand a warm squeeze, and his young friend a big bear hug. 'I've missed you,' Andrew said to him.

'I can tell Andrew is dressed to impress because he has his favourite tie on for you,' Harrison joked with Tanya.

Formalities over, they talked about work for a short while, and then Andrew pulled out an album with photographs of Harrison as an undergraduate. Tanya said she could see the earnest passion in him, even then. Eventually, they got onto the topic of Harrison's mother and Andrew went to get the photograph of her to show to Tanya.

'She's beautiful,' she said, smiling at Harrison. 'I can see her in your eyes.'

Finally, they talked about his crusade to find her killer.

'Are you sure this is worth fighting for?' Andrew asked him. 'Hating someone is like drinking a poison and then waiting for them to die. You've held this inside you for so long. Can you not find a way to let it go? You have a life, a future. Don't let it consume you.'

'I can't let it go yet,' Harrison replied. 'I hear what you're saying, that it's the past. She's gone and nothing I do can bring her back. I understand that, but it's not just about proving she didn't take her own life, because I know for sure now that she didn't. It's not my wishful thinking. But it is about today's victims. If they're threatening us, if they have a network within the police, then that means there are people who are being hurt by them today. I'm going to keep fighting for them.'

Andrew nodded slowly and smiled proudly at the young man he'd mentored and known for most of Harrison's life.

'I won't let it consume me,' Harrison continued. 'I understand now that there are other things worth fighting for, too. But I will not forget her and let her death be for nothing.'

Harrison felt Tanya squeeze his hand encouragingly.

Over the past week, images of the previous year's emotional journey had flashed through his mind. Nunhead Cemetery, Freda Manning's sneering face in the hospice, finding out who his biological father was, then Desmond's cowardly features as he told him his mother had been a police informant and someone powerful had her killed. He'd tried to remember every word of their conversation. Every hint and nuance of language, searching for any clues that might lead him to her killer, but Desmond had been adamant he himself didn't know. Then he'd remembered something that Desmond had said. He'd told him that his mother had gathered evidence, and they thought she had sent it to Harrison.

All this time, he'd assumed that any evidence would have been found and destroyed when they killed her. But what if it hadn't? What if somehow she had sent it to him, or hid it somewhere that she was sure he would find it? He'd gone off the rails after her death. That whole period of his life was a blur until his stepfather had come over from America, tracked him down and got him to pull himself together. After that he'd moved to London and university.

Maybe he shouldn't be looking for an envelope of information, or a key to a safe deposit box. Perhaps he'd been making the most basic mistake all along. He hadn't been thinking like his mother. Every day when he was investigating crimes he tried to imagine the situation at the time of the crime, for both killer and victim. Why had he never done that for his own mother? What would she have done with the limited resources she'd had available? They'd been so close, she understood him, would have anticipated how he thought.

'I wanted to ask if she'd sent you anything at all before she died?' Harrison said. 'I think there's a possibility that whatever evidence she gathered is still out there somewhere. I have to take that slim chance and try to find it.'

'Sent me anything...' Andrew thought for a moment. 'I can't quite remember exactly when, but I think it was just a week or two before I heard about her death. She sent me a postcard.'

Harrison's heart jolted.

'Do you still have it?'

'I'm not sure, but I think so. I think it's in the desk drawer. Give me a minute.'

Andrew disappeared out of the room to his office. They could hear him rummaging around and then his footsteps coming back.

'Here it is. I remember now that I thought it a bit odd because she didn't say anything on it. Just signed it.'

Andrew handed over the postcard. On the back, Harrison recognised his mother's handwriting and saw her signature. Her hand reaching out to him from the past. He flipped the card over. It said *Greetings from Wales*, and was a photograph of a place that he instantly recognised.

'This is it,' he said to them both. 'This is her message telling me where she hid the evidence. We're back in the game.'

A LETTER FROM THE AUTHOR

Many thanks to you for coming this far with Harrison on his journey – I hope you have enjoyed his eighth investigation. If you want to join other readers in hearing all about my new releases and bonus content:

www.stormpublishing.co/gwyn-bennett

Trees featured heavily in this book and they have been a part of so many of our folklore, religions, and spiritual beliefs through the ages. I think there are few things more magnificent and awe-inspiring than an ancient yew or oak tree, and the knowledge that they have been slowly growing for generations of human lives. If only they could talk!

As always, I'd like to not only say thank you to you – the most important element of a reading equation – but also the team who have helped me get this book into your hands. Thank you to everyone at Storm Publishing who have played their role in bringing this latest edition of Harrison's life to you.

If you would like to hear about my new releases, offers, and get a FREE novella telling the story of Harrison's first case in the Ritualistic Behavioural Crime unit, then you can sign up to my readers' club at www.gwynbennett.com. I'd also really appreciate it if you could leave a review on whichever platform you bought this on, and join in the conversation on mine and Storm's social media pages.

Thank you again for spending time with Harrison. Until next time.

Happy Reading,

Gwyn Bennett

www.ingramcontent.com/pod-product-compliance
Lightning Source LLC
Chambersburg PA
CBHW011036190726
48290CB00011B/2867